Kelli leaned back and breathed a long, slow sigh.

"I'm scared because I didn't 'freeze' at the plate. I was just gone—like I was somewhere else, and all of a sudden I came back. And the ball wasn't a fast ball to me—it was floating in. I had nightmares about it for months. I can still see it. That softball, big as some old carnival balloon." She held her hands out in front of her. "And it's floating in to smash my face.

"That's why I'm scared," she concluded. "That's why I don't ever want to go back out there and play again."

KELLI'S CHOICE

DAN JORGENSEN

Chariot Books™
David C. Cook Publishing Co.

Chariot Books is an imprint of David C. Cook Publishing Co.
David C. Cook Publishing Co., Elgin, Illinois 60120
David C. Cook Publishing Co., Weston, Ontario

KELLI'S CHOICE
© 1991 by Dan Jorgensen

Cover design by Bob Fuller
Cover illustration by Quang Ho

Printed in the United States of America
95 94 93 92 91   1 2 3 4 5

Library of Congress Cataloging-in-Publication Data

Jorgensen, Dan.
  Kelli's choice / Dan Jorgensen.
     p.   cm.
  Summary: Kelli is able to overcome her fear, after a serious
accident playing softball, with the help of Herman Hochman,
her senior citizen "assignment."
  ISBN 1-55513-773-3
  [I. Baseball—Fiction. 2. Old age—Fiction. 3. Christian life.]
I. Title.
PZ7.J7688Ke   1991
[Fic]—dc20
                                                90-2693
                                                  CIP
                                                   AC

For my mother and father,
Virginia and Dean Jorgensen,
who instilled in me a sense of fair play
and a love for sports and for life.

Thanks to members of the
St. Olaf College women's softball team
for their assistance and inspiration
in preparing this book.

Contents

CHAPTER ONE

On Edge

KELLI LEANED BACK IN HER CHAIR AND CLOSED HER eyes. Absently she rubbed at the tender spot on her cheek, just below her left eye, and then once again she saw the softball hurtling toward her face. She inhaled sharply and snapped open her eyes. Her best friend, Angie, glanced at her from across the aisle. Kelli read the knowing "You okay?" in Angie's eyes and nodded before returning her attention to the woman speaking at the front of the room.

It was Wednesday night—church night—and the girls were at their high school youth group meeting. The woman, who had turned up unannounced to talk about volunteer youth programs in town, was boring, and Kelli wished she would stop talking and go away. Kelli yawned and shifted her gaze toward their youth group leader, Jared Kinsey. To her surprise, he was staring right at her. She clamped her teeth shut to stifle a yawn. Jared grinned, shook his head, and stood, unwinding his lanky six-foot, six-inch frame until he towered over them all. He strode to the front.

"Well, thank you, Mrs. Coselli, for bringing this information to us." He smiled and extended his hand, which she tentatively shook, taken aback by his abrupt interruption. "I think all your programs sound interesting, but I was especially impressed by the 'foster grandparent' program. I think I'd like to volunteer our little group here to help you out with that one."

A gasp of surprise rippled through the ranks of the twenty students seated before him, and Jared turned and smiled again—this time a wicked little grin that he liked to give them when he knew he had them in a tough spot.

"I know these kids are community-minded and want to do something that will help, and I can't think of anything better than donating a couple hours a week toward making an elderly person feel better. What do you think, gang? You willing to give it a shot?" He gazed out across the group, and Kelli slid down slightly in her chair as he seemed to peer directly at her.

The kids began murmuring among themselves, and Jared held up his hand for quiet. "Kelli?" he asked. "What about you?"

"Uh, well, sure," she mumbled, sitting upright again as Angie giggled at her friend's dilemma.

"And Angie," he added. "How about you?"

Angie reddened and then nodded.

"Great, great! Mrs. Coselli, I'd like you to get me the

names of a couple of these elderly people, and these two girls—Kelli Matthews and Angela Holden—will test this program out for us. If it works for them, then it will be a program that everyone in our group will get involved in."

He gave them all a dazzling smile before taking their guest by the arm and guiding her toward the door. The woman's "thank-yous" could be heard echoing down the hallway as they walked from the room.

"Just what we need," Kelli grumbled, "baby-sitting for some old people in the nursing home. I don't believe he did that to us." Angie nodded in agreement as several of the others snickered. The laughter stopped immediately as Jared re-entered the room.

"Jared," Kelli began, "we can't do this project. What do we know about old people?"

"Senior citizens," he corrected. "You all have grandparents, don't you? Just think of these people as extra grandparents."

"Yeah, but these are *really old* people," Angie anguished. "You heard what she said—most are in their eighties and some even in their nineties. A lot of them can't see or hear well either."

"If I didn't think you could do it, I wouldn't have volunteered you," he said quickly, his voice a little tense. Then he grinned again. "Besides, weren't you the ones telling me just last week how you wanted something really challenging for the spring quarter?" They started to protest, but he interrupted them. "And—" he half-shouted, pausing until they were quiet and then speaking more softly, "and, weren't you the ones saying you wanted to help out good old Fall River, and I should come up with something different so you could do it?"

He stared from person to person as if daring them to tell him he was mistaken. They slowly nodded, and he smiled again.

"Okay then. This is different. And it's challenging. At least I think it is. That's why I want Angie and Kelli to try it for a week and give us a report. If they think it'll work, we'll do it. If not, we'll try something else."

The girls looked at each other before sighing their consent.

"All right." Jared smiled again. "Let's give it a try. That's all for tonight. Let's close in prayer."

After his amen, everyone stood, talking and laughing. Kelli stretched and yawned again while Angie dug under her chair for a notebook. Jared walked over and stood between them. "Tomorrow we'll have a little meeting and talk about this new program. Can you stop over here at three-thirty? I'll be in my office. By then, I should have some names."

The girls looked glumly at each other, and Jared chuckled. "Look, this isn't half as bad as you two think it's going to be. Go into it with a positive attitude and it will be. And, like I said, if it doesn't look good, we'll drop it. Promise." He put a hand on each of their shoulders, and they both smiled in return.

"Sorry to put you on the spot," he added, his rich, mellow voice washing over them. "But you really set yourselves up for it, you know, with that 'I'm bored out of my mind' appearance you were putting on." He turned to Kelli. "Especially you. What's the problem? You look beat."

"I don't know," she said. "Just one of those nights, I guess. It's time for softball season to start, and I always got edgy for a couple of days until practice got going."

"Got going?" he asked. "Aren't you on the team?"

"No, not anymore." Angie started to interrupt, but Kelli gave her a warning look.

Jared saw the exchange. "So, what's the big secret?" he said, glancing from one girl to the other.

"No secret," Kelli replied. "I'm just not on the team."

"But she should be," Angie piped up.

"So, why aren't you?" Jared responded. "What's the deal?"

"Nothing." Kelli glanced at the floor. "It's no deal at all. I used to play, but now I don't. It's as simple as that. But I still get antsy when it's time for the season to begin. Old habits and all. You know?"

"Not really," Jared said. "I've never been much on sports." He leaned his angular frame against the back of Kelli's chair. "So, why should she be on the team, Ang?"

"Because she's good, that's why. Besides, we really need her this year, and she knows it. I've been after her for two weeks to try out, but she's bound and determined to waste her last chance to play. Here it is, our senior year, and one of the best players is going to be sitting in the bleachers." Angie gave Kelli a disparaging glance. "I've gotta go. I've got some homework, and Barringer's throwing a quiz in history first thing. Maybe you can talk some sense into her, Jared. I'll be there tomorrow." She tucked her notebook away and hurried off.

Jared shifted his gaze to Kelli. "Don't worry, I'm not going to try to talk you into anything." He smiled again. "But, if it's something you might want to talk about, I'd be glad to buy you a soda and do some real heavy listening."

Kelli rubbed her hand around her oval-shaped face and ran her fingers through her full, wavy black hair. She returned his smile, her green eyes lighting up her face above a row of bright, even teeth.

"Why not?" She shrugged. "I'm kind of thirsty anyway."

Jared left, jingling some coins in his hand, and was back in minutes with the pop. They plopped down into two front-row chairs.

"So you used to like softball, huh?"

She smiled. "Still do. I played it every day for five years—fifth grade through ninth. I was the best hitter on the team every single year. We were undefeated my freshman year, and basically that same team is back together again this year, except for me. I had my best year ever in ninth grade."

Jared gave her a puzzled glance. "So Angie was right. You were . . . are a good player and you should be on the team. How come you don't want to go back out?"

Kelli took a long drink, then ran her forefinger around the rim of her can. After what seemed like eons, she looked up at Jared. Her eyes were watery, and she

14

swallowed hard.

"I-I know you're going to find this hard to believe, because sometimes I find it hard to believe myself. But, anyway, I guess the reason I don't want to try out for softball anymore is that I-I'm a coward." She took a deep breath. "I'm scared!" A tear finally escaped from the pools in her eyes and trickled past her nose. She swiped at it with the back of her hand, and Jared pulled a tissue from his shirt pocket and handed it over to her.

"Of what?" he asked as she dabbed at her eyes.

"Getting clobbered when I go up to bat." She pushed back her hair again and touched the tender spot below her left eye. "It doesn't show much, but right here is where I got nailed the very last time I played softball— over two years ago. I was standing in, ready to bat, ready to get another big hit like I'd been doing all year. Then, all of a sudden, I seemed to lose my concentration. I don't know what happened or why, but when I finally got my thoughts back on the game, everyone was screaming at me. 'Duck! Duck! Get down!' I looked up and that softball was coming right for my head. It looked huge. And, I-I can't explain it, but I could see it coming at me slow—really slow, you know?"

She stopped her narrative and glanced his direction. He gave her a slight nod, although she wasn't sure if he understood. She tried to explain it again.

"It-it was like . . . slow motion, or something. Really weird. I remember I started to pull away, but then the ball got me. Hard! Right here." She touched the spot again. "Well, when I woke up, I was on a stretcher in an ambulance. The other team's pitcher and my coach were riding with me. I had a broken cheekbone and a concussion. I was in the hospital for three days, and my vision in this eye was blurred for months." She forced a grin. "Pretty weird, looking at things in duplicate every day."

Then she sobered. "But, the weirdest part was that in the ambulance that pitcher kept crying and saying how sorry she was that she let that fast ball get away from her. And the coach kept saying how I might have been all right if I hadn't frozen at the plate like that."

Kelli leaned back and breathed a long, slow sigh. "That's why I'm scared, Jared. That's why I don't want to ever go back out there to play again."

He cleared his throat and started to say something, but she held up a hand and cut him off.

"I'm scared because I didn't freeze at the plate. I was just gone—like I was somewhere else, and all of a sudden I came back. And the ball wasn't a fast ball to me—it was floating in. I had nightmares about it for months. I can still see it. That softball, big as some old carnival balloon." She held out her hands toward him. "And it's floating in to smash my face."

CHAPTER TWO

Decisions

FALL RIVER WAS A PLEASANT LITTLE FARMING COM-
munity in the heart of the Cooper River Valley. It also
was in the exact center of a 120-mile circle which included eight other communities that, along with Fall
River, made up the Class AA River Valley Conference.

By virtue of its location, Fall River should have been
the largest city in the valley. But by some quirk of fate,
the major highways had skirted the fringes of the valley,
leaving all eight of the neighboring communities larger
and faster-growing. And as the communities grew, so
did their schools, while Fall River slipped farther
behind. Now the "orphan" of the conference, its enroll-
ment was barely over 400, while the smallest of its
neighbors, Rocky Ford, had grown to nearly 650. Next
year, Fall River's conference ties would end. Even worse,
the Fall River school board had voted to drop the minor
sports, including softball.

So, as the athletic director liked to keep reminding the Fall River athletic teams—this was it! This was the last chance to take home a trophy in the RVC and get into the prestigious large school state tournaments. Next year, they'd not only drop out of the RVC but into the Class A division.

This was their Cinderella year but, unfortunately, the glass slipper hadn't fit. One by one, the FRHS teams had gone down in defeat. There were just two chances left, softball and baseball, and the baseball team didn't look like much of a contender.

But softball! That was another story. This group of seniors had played together since seventh grade, starting slowly but steadily improving. As sophomores they had finished fourth in the RVC and third in the district play-offs. Last year, as juniors, they had taken second in both the RVC and districts. Only powerful Point Pleasant, the "giant" of the Valley schools, had barred their path to a state play-off berth. If there was to be "a year" for this team, it was going to be this one—the final year for softball in Fall River. Other girls in town had argued long and hard to keep the program going, but budget cuts were mandatory, especially in a community that relied on agriculture. The money just wasn't there.

All eight starting fielders were back and so was the team's best pitcher, Kari Jamison. A new girl named Becky Randall was rumored to be a pitcher, too, and a good one at that. Everything was in place. They might close down the softball program, but this team would go out with a bang!

Then tragedy struck. A few weeks earlier, starting catcher Paulette Stoddard had been injured in a car crash. She wouldn't be back on her feet until early May, and even then she wouldn't be well enough to play. Her loss left a big, big hole in the lineup, and it was that hole which the delegation of players intended to fill as they surrounded the lunch table where Kelli and Angie sat.

Kari was leading the group and settled down directly opposite Kelli. The other three were Samantha Turner, Rayanne Trent, and Melanie Postma, the starting infielders at first, second, and third base, respectively. Everyone called them "the guys" because they preferred the shortened versions of their names—Sam, Ray, and Mel—and they were always in a joking mood.

At least, almost always. Now they all looked grim.

Kelli looked up, surprised. "Hi," she said in a muffled voice as she gulped down a large bite of her sandwich. "What's up?" Her last two words came out a bit clearer as she laid the rest of the sandwich on her tray.

"We want you to come out for the team," Kari said quickly, after exchanging glances with her three partners. "We've had a team meeting, and everyone voted to ask you to join. We want you to be the catcher."

Kelli's mouth dropped open. "What? A team meeting? Softball hasn't even started yet, so how could you have a team meeting?"

"Okay, it wasn't a full team meeting and it wasn't official, okay?" Sam spoke sharply, in a voice totally out of character for the happy-go-lucky "class clown."

"It wasn't official, but it was the seniors. All of us—

even Paulette," Mel chipped in, stopping suddenly at the slight exclamation of surprise on Kelli's part. "We met in her hospital room yesterday after school. We decided that if we're really going to have a chance to make state this year, we need a good catcher. That's you."

"Come on," Kelli began, an incredulous sound to her voice and an equally incredulous expression on her face. "I'm not a catcher, and I haven't even picked up a softball in two years!"

"Doesn't matter," Kari said. "We all know you're a natural when it comes to softball, and you were the catcher in seventh and eighth grade. You only moved over to shortstop when Paulette got to be such a good hitter and the coach decided to put her at catcher."

Kelli shrugged. "Okay, so I used to catch. That doesn't change anything. I haven't played for over two years, and I don't think I can anymore. Simple as that." She took a huge bite from her sandwich and stared silently at her tray as she chewed, hoping her silence would signify an end to the conversation.

"Be stubborn then," Ray inserted. "But you're a good player, and we know you can do the job for us. The new coach'll be willing to give you a shot at it right from the start, because she doesn't know anything about what happened before. All we're asking is that you come out and try. If it doesn't work out, you can quit."

"Come on, whaddaya say?" Angie asked, grabbing Kelli's arm.

"I say how come you never told me about this meeting yesterday?" Kelli answered, an edge to her voice. "You knew about this last night, Angie. Some friend you are."

Angie looked at her tray. "I-I told the guys I wouldn't say anything till today. Everyone wanted to talk to you about it together."

"Gang up on me, you mean?" Kelli glared as she spoke. She munched on a carrot while the others sat silently watching. Finally she threw up her hands in despair.

"Even if I came out, what makes you think the coach would put me in as a starter?"

"Who else do we have?" Sam said seriously. The way it sounded brought a round of laughter from everyone, including Kelli.

She thought. "Well, there's Lara."

"Sure, but she's only a freshman, and she lets about every third pitch get by her," Kari replied. "Who knows, maybe she'll be great. But we could end up losing a lot of games before she gets settled in, and you know as well as I do that the team's record is the final factor in selecting teams for the play-offs. Only the top two in the conference get in, and we could lose a lot of games right off the bat and be finished before we even get started."

"You might do that with me, too, you know," Kelli said quietly. "Who says I can still catch a ball?"

Kari shrugged. "Who knows you can't? All we're asking is that you give it a chance. You may not believe in yourself, but we all believe in you."

Kelli picked up her spoon and stirred it around in her fruit cocktail for a few seconds. "I don't know," she said

21

at last. "I'll have to think about it."

"Okay, but don't think too long. Practice starts Thursday and we need you," Mel said. "We know you can do the job for us, Kelli. It's time you gave yourself a chance."

Kelli angrily crumpled the slip of paper into a ball. First the ball team, now this. "What a day," she sighed. She pulled her arm back to throw the paper into a near-by trash can, but in mid-toss she stopped. Slowly she smoothed out the paper, revealing a badly wrinkled typewritten name.

"Jared!" she admonished the air, glaring at nothing in particular. "What have you gotten me into?" She stared down at the paper as she walked slowly toward the brick building just ahead.

"Herman Hochman, age eighty-eight, Fall River Nursing Home."

She read the name aloud for the umpteenth time and then stared up at the main entry way to the home, breaking out in a cold sweat as she did so.

"This is crazy," she said, scuffing her feet from side-to-side. "What am I going to say to an eighty-eight-year-old man? Besides, he's probably bedridden or in a wheelchair. Probably doesn't even want anyone visiting him. They should've given me a woman. What am I going to say to an old man?"

"May I help you? Are you looking for someone?"

The voice startled her, and Kelli jumped slightly as its owner—a pleasant looking woman in her mid-forties—walked up to her.

"I'm sorry," she apologized. "I didn't mean to startle you, but you looked as though you were lost." The woman was dressed in a business suit and wore a name tag indicating that she was employed at the home.

"Oh, no. Uh, I mean, it's okay. I'm not lost, just debating whether or not I should go in." Kelli managed a half-hearted smile.

"Well, whom are you looking for? Maybe I can be of assistance."

"Yeah, maybe. I was, uh," she paused. "I was thinking of dropping in to see a Mr. Hochman. You don't know him, do you?"

The woman's questioning expression changed to one of delight.

"Herman Hochman? Yes, indeed. He's a delightful man." Then her smile changed to a slight frown. "But he's been on a bit of a downward slide the last couple of months, I'm sorry to say. Poor old man. He doesn't have any family around these parts, and he gets so few visitors. He could certainly use some company."

"I'm going to visit him on the foster grandparents program. Have you heard of that?" Kelli asked hopefully. "I mean, it's, uh, okay for me to visit him, isn't it?"

"Of course it is, Miss—" the woman stopped.

"Matthews." Kelli swallowed hard. "Kelli Matthews. I'm from the senior youth group at Bethel Church over on Tenth Street. We're just getting started in this grandparents program, and I got Mr. Hochman's name for a visit. We're kind of testing it out to see if it's going to work—if you know what I mean?"

The woman smiled again. "Of course. Well, I'm Marilyn Horner, and I try to help keep things in order here at the home. I'm very pleased that you're willing to give the program a try. So few young people come in here that it's depressing sometimes even for me." She looked around as if she was afraid of being heard and then added in a slightly lower voice, "And I get to go home at the end of the day." She extended her hand as she chuckled, and Kelli relaxed and laughed in response, taking the woman's hand and looking closer at her name tag. In small letters under the name it had the title "Administrator in Charge."

Marilyn opened the main door and gestured inside. "As I said, Herman gets very few visitors, and he's been depressed lately."

"How come?" Kelli found herself moving inside despite her apprehension.

"His best friend here for many years was a man named John Paulson. John had a stroke about six months ago, and three months ago he died. I think part of Herman died then, too, and he just hasn't been the same since. In fact, we've had some trouble getting him to come out of his room except for meals. He could use a good, friendly visit from a nice young person like yourself."

Kelli swallowed again and nodded, trying to imagine what an eighty-eight-year-old man who wouldn't come out of his room looked like. She barely heard the woman's conversation as they moved down a hallway, and suddenly they were stopped before a doorway with Herman's name on it. Marilyn knocked a couple of times and then opened the door and ushered Kelli in.

"Herman, you've got a guest," she said in a normal voice. That surprised Kelli, who had been thinking she'd need to speak louder than usual in order to be heard. The old man was sitting in a chair next to his bed, his television on. Kelli couldn't tell whether he was watching it or not. He made no response except to turn his head slightly in their direction. "This is Kelli Matthews," the administrator continued. "She's just come by to say hello and talk for a few minutes."

Marilyn turned to Kelli and put a hand on her shoulder. "Well, I'll just leave you here. You can stay as long as you like, although you should know that we go to dinner at five forty-five." She glanced at her watch. "It's about five now, so you can take a half hour or so. Is that okay?"

"Oh, er, sure, that'll be fine," Kelli said, embarrassed because she wasn't sure she'd stay much longer than five or ten minutes. Marilyn smiled again, then slipped from the room, leaving Kelli standing awkwardly just inside the door. She stood there silently surveying the room, aware that the old man was not really acknowledging her presence. She mustered her courage and took a few more steps inside.

"My name's Kelli," she began, "but I guess you already heard that, huh?" She giggled nervously and felt like kicking herself for it. "You mind if I sit down here?" She gestured toward another chair at the foot of the bed, and the man gave a slight nod which she hoped meant that it was okay. She settled into the chair and glanced up at the television. "So, whatcha watchin'?"

He shifted slightly in the chair and when he spoke, the gravelly sound in his voice caused Kelli to stir uneasily.

"Not really watching. Just got it on to have something on." He wheezed a little and then coughed twice. "Do I know you?" He eyed her suspiciously.

Kelli shook her head. "I just heard you hadn't had anybody visiting for a while, and I thought I'd come over, that's all. Thought maybe we could talk or something." She looked closer at him as she spoke. He was stoop-shouldered and nearly bald with heavy, horn-rimmed glasses and lots of wrinkles across his cheeks and forehead. She couldn't tell for sure, but he appeared to be tall, or at least was tall at one time.

He wheezed again and gazed back at the TV. After what seemed like minutes, he turned back toward her. "Don't really know what we can talk about." He stopped, gasped, and began coughing. It was disturbing, and Kelli half turned away in disgust. "Sorry," he finally continued. "Get these coughing spells all the time these days."

They sat without speaking for a couple more minutes, and Kelli tried to focus in on the television show. It was some game show, but she didn't know which one. Finally, she coughed herself and stood. "Well, look, I'd probably better get going. Just thought I'd stop and say hello." She started to turn toward the door.

"Could you pull back the curtains for me? I mean, before you leave . . . if that's okay?" His voice sounded weaker, and he didn't turn away from the television as he spoke.

"Sure," Kelli said, nodding and moving toward the lone window, which was mostly covered by a dark curtain.

She pulled the curtains wide, allowing the sunlight to stream in. "Pretty nice day today," she said, trying to think of what else she could say before leaving. He nodded but didn't reply. Staring out the window, she added, "I used to love early spring days like this because I knew the weather was just right for getting back on the field."

"You a farm girl?" His quick response and obvious note of interest caught her off-guard, and she turned with a laugh.

"Me? No! No, nothing like that," she laughed again. "Actually, it was the ball field—softball—I meant. Whenever the nice spring days arrived, it was only a matter of a few more days until practice began . . . time to get ready for another season."

"Oh," he chuckled himself, and Kelli watched the wrinkles form neat lined patterns away from the corners of his eyes and mouth. "I use ta farm, so the spring days always got me thinking about getting back to the field, too."

She grinned and nodded.

"Course, I use ta play a little ball myself, too. Baseball was my game, though. Never had much time for softball." He sat up a little straighter and stared toward the window, past Kelli's shoulder. "Long time ago." He shook his head and sighed. "Yep, real long time ago when I played. More'n sixty years now, I guess."

Kelli walked back to the chair and pulled it closer to his. "You play very much?"

"Yeah, I suppose I did."

"Really? What position?"

"Outfield," he coughed again but not as hard. "Played all over the outfield and I pitched some, too. Yeah, tried a little pitching from time to time. Guess I did." A little smile flickered across his face and those beautiful wrinkle lines reappeared. "Some people thought I was pretty good, I guess." He eyed the window, then stirred. "Come over here and give me a hand," he demanded. "I think I'd like to take a look out the window."

"Sure," Kelli jumped up and hurried to his side, helping him first to his feet and then awkwardly over to the window. He stood staring outside, leaning against her for support.

"You're right," he finally spoke. "It's pretty nice outside. Would be a good day to get out and start working out. You still playing?"

Kelli shook her head. "No. I haven't played for a couple years."

"You quit?" He stepped back and gave her a stern look. "Didn't like it?"

"Oh no, nothing like that," she responded. "I got hurt."

"Knee or elbow or something?"

"No." Now it was her turn to stare out the window and she reached up with her left hand and touched the tender spot as she replied.

He ignored the gesture and continued his stern expression. "Well, if it weren't a knee or a elbow, then you should still be able to play, unless—" he looked her over more closely. "You too old to play?"

Coming from him it sounded silly, and they both realized it. Kelli laughed first and the old man joined in, his wheezing laugh interrupted by a cough or two but genuine in its intensity. He slipped back to his chair, this time unattended, and Kelli slowly returned to her own and sat down. He was waiting now, expectantly, his expression demanding an explanation for her not playing.

"I got hit in the face by a pitch." She touched the spot again and his gaze followed her hand as she slowly rubbed the spot. "About here. Still hurts some when the weather changes."

"My joints all do that," he nodded. " 'Cept for me, it's the arthritis and rheumatism. I think you're probably too young for that."

"Yeah," she agreed. "I guess so."

"You like to play?" She saw him shift forward in his chair. She realized that he really wanted to know.

"Yes, I did. I miss it a lot."

"So, you should go back. You *are* still in school, ain't ya?"

She nodded.

"Don't let bein' scared get in your way. You'll always wonder if you maybe shoulda taken the chance."

There was a knock on the door, and a nurse poked her head in, speaking as she entered. "Time for dinner now, Mr. Hochman. You'll have to get up and—" She halted, startled at seeing Kelli in the room. Obviously, the administrator hadn't told anyone about her visit. Kelli jumped to her feet, and the old man slowly stood beside her.

"What time is it?" Kelli asked.

"It's five-thirty," the nurse said. "Who are you?"

"Kelli," she said. She walked over and held out her hand to the old man. "I've got to go now, Mr. Hochman. It was nice talking with you."

He took her hand, and his felt frail and wispy in hers. "It was nice talking to you, too, Kelli. I hope you give that team of yours a try. Remember what I said."

She nodded. "Yeah, well . . ." she paused. "Guess I'll have to see." She turned and hurried to the door, but his voice stopped her.

"You coming back to visit again?"

There was a hopeful sound to his voice, and Kelli looked back over her shoulder. Already, he looked different from when she had arrived.

"Yeah." She said it with a small half-laugh. "Yeah, I guess I might sometime." She grinned and gave him a little wave before hurrying away.

CHAPTER THREE

Safe at Home

KELLI SLIPPED IN THROUGH THE KITCHEN DOOR AND nearly ran over her mother who was hurrying out.

"Oh, Kelli! I didn't hear you coming through the garage." Mrs. Matthews paused to catch her breath.

"Sorry, Mom. Hey, where are you going? Isn't it about time to eat?"

"Yes, but your father just called from the office and asked if I could pick him up. He had to work late, and now his car won't start—vapor lock or something. Can you go get him?"

"No problem." Kelli skipped out through the garage, hopped into their second car, a beat-up old Chevy, and started away. Ten minutes later, she pulled up in front of her dad's office.

"Hi," he greeted her with a smile. "Mom said you weren't home."

"Walked in just after you called," she said, checking

over her shoulder and then backing the car away from the curb. "What's wrong?"

"I don't know," he said, an exasperated sound to his voice. "This new car has been nothing but trouble since we got it. Ralph thought it was vapor locked, and I'm not even sure what that means. In any case, the garage sent over a tow truck." He patted the dash of the car. "Thankfully this old thing keeps on going. Kind of like an old horse we had back on the farm."

Kelli's dad liked to talk about his childhood days on a nearby farm, particularly when something was going wrong. To stop an old story that she'd heard plenty of times before, Kelli started talking first.

"Dad, I've got a couple of questions for you."

He straightened his briefcase at his feet, checked his seat belt and nodded. "Fire away."

"Some of the kids at school have been after me to go out for softball, and—" she paused as she pulled up to a stop sign, checked traffic both ways, and then drove on. "And, anyway, I've been trying to decide what to do."

"Do you want to play?" He said it softly, a note of concern in his voice.

"That's just it . . . I do and I don't. You know what I mean?"

He sighed. "Yes, I suppose I do. I've been faced with decisions like that from time to time. No matter what you decide, you always wonder if you would've been better off taking the other choice." He drummed his fingers on the dash for a few seconds, staring off into the northern sky as the mid-March evening shadows deepened around them. There were a few small drifts remaining beside the streets, but most of the snow had melted away. Finally, he looked in Kelli's direction as she turned off the main route and headed down the side street toward home.

"You know I've always supported you in whatever you've tried to do." Kelli nodded and he continued. "This thing about softball has been a tough one for your mother and me, because we know how much you loved it and how well you were doing before . . . before you got hurt. Are you asking me to make a decision for you on this?"

"I don't know," she said as she pulled the car into the driveway. "I guess I just wonder if you think I should try it again or not, that's all."

"Well," he began.

"And there's more," Kelli interrupted him. "Do you know a guy over in the nursing home named Herman Hochman?"

"Herman Hochman?" Dad looked puzzled. He pondered the name for a few moments. "Oh, yes! Herman Hochman. He was an old farmer . . . lived about ten miles outside of town. I haven't seen him for several years, though. What do you know about him?"

"I met him this afternoon," Kelli said. "He's my new foster grandparent through our church youth program."

"Guess I hadn't heard about that," her dad replied. "But what's he got to do with playing softball?"

"Nothing," Kelli responded, "except he said

something to me that has had me thinking for the last hour that maybe I should go back out. He said I shouldn't let being scared get in my way of taking a chance—not if I liked what I was taking the chance on. Does that make sense?"

"Yes, it does."

"That's what I thought. As I walked back from the nursing home, I thought *I can stay safe at home and not worry about being hurt in softball because I'm not play-ing it. Or, I can go out for a sport I really enjoy—even though I might get hurt again. Maybe I'll even do a good job and help my team win a championship.* I'm scared, Dad, but I want to take a chance. I don't want to be safe at home."

"Except when you slide into home plate to score," her father said. "Safe!" He gestured with his arms like an umpire.

Kelli laughed. "I guess I'll go do something really dumb and give it a try."

"Good," Dad said, unsnapping his seat belt and open-ing the car door. "Guess you really didn't need to talk to me after all. Now shut off the car before we run out of gas and I have to pay a towing charge on this one, too."

They walked arm in arm into the house, but in the pit of her stomach, Kelli felt a million butterflies unfolding their wings.

"This is it? Eleven girls?" Miss McGuire, the new coach, tapped at her clipboard and paced back and forth. "Good grief, eleven girls! How do they expect me to make a team out of so few players?" She spoke as if they weren't there; then she turned and spoke directly to the girls assembled before her in the Fall River High School gym. "Do you know Point Pleasant has sixty girls out for varsity softball? Sixty! Good grief." She turned around again, muttering, "Nine seniors, a junior, and a freshman. I don't believe it!"

"Uh, Coach?" It was Sam.

The new coach glanced at her clipboard for a second, matching up Sam's practice jersey number with her name and number on the board. "Yes," she said irritably, "what is it, Samantha?"

The rest of the girls broke into laughter, but quieted quickly at a glaring stare from Miss McGuire.

"Sam," Sam replied. "Or maybe Sammy. Only my grandmother calls me Samantha."

The coach cracked a smile for the first time since they had started the meeting. "Okay, Sam. What is it you wanted to say?"

Sam stood up. At five-foot-eleven, she was the team's biggest player. With her bright orange-red hair and intense blue eyes, she could look imposing when she wanted to. She was the only "freckle-less" redhead Kelli had ever met.

Generally Sam was a prankster, but now she was deadly serious. "We already know that Point Pleasant and probably every other school in the River Valley Conference has at least forty players out," she began, "so you don't have to tell us about that. And we don't have any sophomores because they figure what's the use, you know? Next year no team, so why beat your brains out playing this time around? But we've got us." She gestured toward her teammates. "I count eleven. Don't those other teams play nine at a time, same as we do?"

Coach McGuire stared hard at her for a few seconds. "Absolutely," she said at last, breaking the tension, "and it was stupid of me to forget that."

"That's good," Sam responded, then her pale complexion reddened in embarrassment. "Uh, I mean, I don't mean that it's good that you said you were stupid," she stammered. "I-I meant, it's good that the others don't put any more on the field at one time than we do, because . . ." she stopped to catch her breath, and the rest of the team began to laugh. "What I mean," she half-shouted as they laughed even harder, "is that the rest of this conference doesn't have eleven players as good as our eleven, and they definitely aren't going to put a better nine on the field than we are."

The girls laughed and applauded.

"You're weird, Sam," Angie inserted as the laughter died. "But since you hit the ball so well, we're going to let you stay."

"And who might you be?" the coach interrupted as Sam swung her cap in Angie's direction.

"I'm Angie," she answered, her wide-set eyes and pug nose accented by her smile. "Angie Holden. I play right field."

"She means she stands around in right field," another girl chimed in. "Generally I stop the ball in the infield before it gets to her."

"Just a minute." The coach dropped her clipboard to her side and held up her hands. "Why don't you all just tell me who you are—one at a time. Okay?" She nodded and pointed to Rayanne, who had identified her position as an infielder. "We might as well go on with you."

"I'm Rayanne Trent, but you can call me Ray."

"Ray's just one of the guys," Kari Jamison said. Giggling erupted among the team members, and the coach appeared confused. Kari stepped forward. "I'm Kari Jamison," she said, brushing her hair out of her eyes. "I do a little pitching."

"Very little," Ray shot back. "We save her, too," she said, turning to the coach. "I play second base; Sam's got first; and Mel's over at third. We let Krissie take shortstop because Kris could be either a guy's or a girl's name."

"Wait a minute, wait a minute!" the coach said, waving her hands in despair. "You have me totally confused now. Who's Mel . . . and who's Krissie?"

"I'm Mel . . . Melanie Postma." Another red-headed girl, nearly as tall as Sam, stood and waved a hand in the coach's direction. She stepped up beside Sam and Ray. With her deep red hair brushed back and in a full perm, she almost looked taller than the big first baseman. Together they made Ray, who was just five-three, look like a shrimp. Ray suddenly jumped ahead of them, her white-blonde pixie cut hair bouncing.

"I'm getting away from them," she explained to the

startled coach. "Every time I get between those two, I feel like they're going to use me for a wishbone or something."

A black girl with a mass of tight curls stood. "I'm Kris." There was an edge to her voice, and she scowled slightly. "Sometimes I get called Krissie, but I prefer to be called Kris. Kris Gillespie."

The coach nodded. "So," she said, "I've got an infield made up of 'guys,' with redheads at the corners."

Sam and Mel glanced at each other and exchanged a hand slap as Kris sat back down. Another girl stood.

"I'm Darcy Penski." She spoke quietly, and the rest of the team eyed her with respect. Her olive complexion was flawless, and her tight, curly hair was similar in appearance to Kris's. She, too, was tall and slender. Her oval eyes were an intense green. "I play center field." The coach's gaze shifted to the next row.

"I'm Beth Chapman. My friends call me Chappy." A bouncy girl with a lop-sided grin and sleepy-looking eyes was speaking. "I play left field," she paused, "and sometimes bench; depends on—" She sat down quickly as the others laughed.

"On what?" Coach McGuire responded.

"On Julie," Beth said, pointing down to the front where another black girl sat with a sheepish smile. "Sometimes she's just playing better than me."

Julie stood up, twisting her cap and glancing around nervously. "I-I'm Julie Stevens." She shrugged.

"Julie's a little shy sometimes." It was Becky Randall speaking. She put a hand on Julie's shoulder. "I'm

Becky. I'm new here this year and I guess I'm your other pitcher." Becky was almost a twin to Kari in her appearance and the coach, noticing the resemblance, glanced quickly over at the other pitcher in surprise. "Yeah, I know," she said, noticing the coach's reaction. "We've been getting confused a lot. We look alike, but that's about it. She's left-handed and I'm right, and we're *not* related. Besides, I'm a junior, and juniors rule, as everyone knows!"

She stuck her tongue out at Kari, laughed and bowed as the seniors booed, then dodged a wadded up piece of paper which the other pitcher flung her direction. The paper ball was stopped neatly by a heavyset girl with wavy auburn hair and glasses. She stood up and nodded toward the coach while tossing the paper back to Kari.

"She's one of our catchers," Kari said quickly. "Guess that's easy to see, huh?"

The coach rolled her eyes.

"I'm Lara Nolan," the catcher said. "I'm your one freshman. I'm trying to get a couple of my friends interested. They just didn't think they'd have much of a chance to play this year, you know, with, uh . . ." she paused, swallowed hard, then continued, "with such a good group of seniors playing ahead of them."

The coach gave her an understanding smile. "Okay, Lara. Glad to have you out. How come you decided to give it a try?"

Lara shrugged. "Guess I thought I'd get a chance to play some, until, uh . . ." she stopped again and glanced over her shoulder at Kelli, who felt her face reddening as not only Lara but every other girl looked her direction.

"Don't worry," Kelli said, standing. "You'll probably get lots of playing time." She laughed nervously and then wondered why she was being so dorky. *Why did I ever let them talk me into this? Why did I talk myself into this?* She shook her head, realizing she was being spoken to. "Uh, what?" she said aloud. "I didn't understand the question."

Everyone laughed as the coach gave her a quizzical look. "I said, what's your name?"

"Oh." Kelli grew redder. "Kelli. Kelli Matthews. I'll be trying out for catcher, I guess." She sat down, wishing she could sink through the bleacher seats and out of sight.

CHAPTER FOUR

Fresh Start

AFTER A HALF HOUR OF RUNNING, STRETCHING, AND throwing, the reality of being on the softball team came back in a hurry. It was hard work. The rapidly changing late March weather didn't help matters either. It had been sunny and mild when they started; now it was clouding over and a nippy wind had picked up.

The girls were paired up, tossing the ball back and forth to each other while the coach jotted something on a piece of paper. "Okay, everybody in here!" she suddenly shouted, glancing at her clipboard and blowing her whistle to get their attention.

"We're going to practice some quick starts to first base, then I want each of you to jog over to third and practice coming down the third base line and sliding into home plate." Coach McGuire raised her voice slightly to make herself heard over the rising wind.

"Just start at home plate, pretend to swing, and then

41

sprint to first. I want to see how quick you are. Once you get over to third, take off at my signal, pretend I'm the catcher, and give me your best slide past me into home. Got it?"

They nodded and hurried over to home plate, which was surrounded by damp sand just recently raked out by the school's grounds crew. Sam jumped to the front of the line and Kelli and Lara hung back, taking up the last two positions as the coach moved out about halfway between home plate and the pitcher's rubber.

"Okay!" she shouted. "Go!"

Sam did her best imitation of a majestic swing, leisurely dropped her imaginary bat at her side, and stood staring toward left field. Then she leaped up, punched her fist into the air, and took a couple of jogging steps toward first.

"Hold it!" the coach shouted, hurrying forward. "What's going on?"

"I'm a natural home run hitter," Sam said, trying to keep a serious expression on her face while her teammates were breaking up. "That one was gone. A clean home run."

The coach turned away for a few seconds, obviously fighting to control a smile. "That's real nice, Sam. But let's say, just for the sake of practice, that you topped that one instead, and it's slowly rolling toward third. Now what're you planning to do?"

"Get moving, of course!" Sam shouted. She exchanged her smug smile for a shocked expression, spun around, and sprinted hard toward first while the coach

42

snapped on the stopwatch and shook her head.

"Just in case any of the rest of you are 'natural' home run hitters," Miss McGuire announced, "let me warn you that anything hit out of the infield will cost you two laps around the entire field." She swept her arm in a circle encompassing the whole complex to make her point as the girls grinned and began jumping up and down to keep warm.

"Darn, there goes about my only chance to hit a homer," Beth said between chattering teeth. "Leave it to Sam to spoil it for everyone."

Each girl hustled through the drill, and when the line reached Lara and Kelli, Kelli stepped back and nudged the freshman in ahead of her. Lara had a good stance at the plate, but when she started running it was obvious she was the slowest member of the team. Then it was Kelli's turn to take her imaginary bat and stand in. Shaking, she stepped forward and waited for the coach to raise her hand. It seemed like every girl—even those jogging behind the coach toward third base—had stopped talking or moving to see what Kelli would do.

Kelli half-crouched, pulled her hands back as if holding the bat, and watched the coach's hand come down. Then she saw the ball. Just like before, it was floating in from the coach, coming right at her. She uttered a little cry and ducked sharply, pulling both hands up to her head.

Coach McGuire rushed forward along with several of the others, with Angie in the lead.

"Kelli? You all right?" asked the coach.

Kelli looked up at Miss McGuire's concerned face and saw that Angie was about to speak. She held up her hand. "No-nothing. I-I had a sharp pain in my neck. Something like that. I-I don't know what it was." She shook her head and signaled to Angie to keep quiet.

Her friend backed away a couple of steps.

"I'm fine now. Let's try it again."

The coach eyed her, concern in her face. "Are you sure?"

Kelli forced a smile. "No problem. Just give me a minute or two to work out the kink in my neck. Maybe you can have a couple of the girls start the drill from third base, then I'll be ready." She pretended to rub her neck and turned her back to the coach, glancing at Angie and noting the worry on her friend's face. "Really," she said, turning quickly back to the coach. "I'm starting to work it out already. The muscle must've tightened up in the cold. I'm not in very good shape yet," she added apologetically.

Coach McGuire walked over and patted her on the shoulder. "Okay. Just move back away from the plate for a few minutes, and when you're ready you can give it a try." She gave Kelli a reassuring smile, then blew her whistle to start the third-to-home drill.

Kelli backed away, absently rubbing at her neck even though she knew that part of what she'd said was a lie. She'd frozen again! What was going on? How could she overcome this fear? She turned toward the bleachers set up along the first base side behind home plate and was surprised to see two people sitting there, bundled up

44

against the chill. One of them waved to her and then gestured for Kelli to come over. She jogged over toward them, her expression changing from confusion to recognition as she drew closer. She smiled brightly.

"Mr. Hochman!" she exclaimed. She glanced at his companion. It was the administrator from the home. "And, uh," Kelli paused, embarrassed. "I'm sorry, I don't know if you're Miss Horner or Mrs. Horner."

"Marilyn," the woman replied. "Just call me Marilyn." She held tightly to the arm of the old man, whose face was red from the cold wind. "I had to bring Herman out here today, in spite of this miserable change of weather," she continued, glancing at the sky which had become even cloudier as the winds increased. "He told me you might be trying out, and he was bound and determined to get here to cheer you on."

Kelli gave him a radiant smile. "Thanks." She pointed back toward the field. "As you can see, it's not too hard to make this team. We barely have enough players."

"So you're going to give it a try?" he said, his voice sounding gravelly.

"Yeah, I guess. Maybe." She hung her head slightly.

"Kelli! You ready?" The coach's shout interrupted them and Kelli turned back toward her to reply. Nearly all of the girls had run the third-to-home drill.

"I'll be right there!" she shouted. She turned back to Mr. Hochman. "I've got to try a couple of things. I had a little trouble first time up. I'm supposed to pretend to swing and then see how fast I can get to first." She reached up and touched the area where her neck met her

45

shoulder. "Think I must have pulled a muscle or something. But it's okay now." She looked sheepishly at the old man, and his weathered face registered disapproval. Kelli knew he didn't believe her.

"We wondered what happened," Marilyn responded. "We got here just before that."

Kelli stared at him. So, he'd seen what happened. Well, who was he to judge? Suddenly she was angry at him. What business did he have being out here anyway? She started to turn away when his rumbling voice stopped her.

"Set your feet, lean in, and don't think about the ball. Just get set and take a practice chop. Chop at it. Remember, you're only working on your running now."

"Okay, sure." She nodded and hurried back to home plate, still angry at him for interfering. Who did he think he was, anyway? Good grief, they'd only met once.

"You ready to run?"

The coach's voice snapped her out of her thoughts. "Yeah. Ready," she said, an edge to her voice.

"Good. Since everyone else is finished, I want you to run to first, hustle on over to third, and come on back home with a slide. Don't worry about your time from third to home. I'm more interested in seeing how well you slide."

Kelli stepped up to the plate, glanced quickly over at the bleachers where the old man stood watching, and dug her heels into the soft sand. The coach raised her arm and Kelli leaned toward the plate, her arms cocked back as if she were holding a bat. Even in the biting cold, she could feel beads of perspiration begin to form on her brow.

"Please, God," she said softly, "help me." She took her eyes off the coach and stared toward first. Suddenly, the coach's whistle broke the silence. Kelli chopped down and dug toward first at full speed. It seemed like eternity, but she crossed the bag, looped around toward second and sprinted on. She hit that bag at full speed and accelerated as she pounded toward third. All other thoughts were gone. Her heart thumped wildly and she saw her teammates standing like statues just beyond home plate.

Kelli reached third and headed down the line toward home plate. Out of the corner of her eye, she saw the coach come into view, hurrying toward the plate as if she were the catcher about to tag her out. Kelli jumped slightly in the air, threw her body sideways and hit the soft sand with a full slide. She watched the coach go past and realized she had finished the slide across home plate. Suddenly, she was surrounded by the others, all cheering and pounding her on the back as they helped her to her feet.

Angie grabbed her by both shoulders and shook her hard. "Kelli! You did it! I prayed you'd stand in there and swing, and you did it!"

"So did I!" Kelli matched Angie's excitement with her own.

"And run!" Angie added. "Good grief, girl! I haven't seen you run like that since you ran away from John Hedges when he tried to kiss you in eighth grade." Kelli gave Angie a shove, but Angie reached out and grabbed her friend by the arm.

"Hey, gang!" She took in all the others in a glance. "Kelli's back! Now I know we're going all the way to the championship!"

They all cheered and then stood back as Kelli moved out of their circle back toward home plate.

Coach McGuire was staring in amazement at her stopwatch. Kelli grinned at her teammates, brushed the sand from her uniform and stepped gingerly toward the coach. "Well," she said, "how'd I do?"

"Not bad," the coach said, emitting a low whistle in the process. "You always run the bases that well?"

"I don't know," she answered. "It's been a while since I tried."

The coach looked up sharply, a puzzled expression on her face. "That so? Didn't you play last year?"

"No. Not since my freshman year," Kelli said.

"Why not?"

"Just didn't feel like it, I guess." She gulped and forced a smile. "But I'm feeling like it now. So, guess I'm ready to go, huh?"

"I said you ran the bases well," Coach McGuire replied. "How's your hitting? That didn't look like much of a swing to me."

"I wasn't really trying to—" she paused. "That is, I was just taking someone's advice on how to swing without getting that cramp back in my neck. That's all." She turned and looked toward the seats, but Mr. Hochman and Marilyn were gone.

"I'm probably just a little rusty is all," she said, turning back to the coach. "I guess I hit about .340, maybe .350, the last time I played. If I can get back in the groove, maybe I can do that again. Maybe even .400. Who knows?"

"Sure. Who knows?" the coach said in a slightly mocking voice. She smiled to herself and slowly shook her head as she reset the watch and turned away. "Catcher, right?" She spun around as she asked the question.

"Who, me?" Kelli said, caught off guard by the coach's sudden move.

"Yes, you. Of course, you. You were catcher last year—I mean, last time you were out? When you were a freshman?"

Kelli shook her head. "Uh, no. Shortstop." She quickly held up her hand as the coach's mouth dropped open. "But I don't want to try out there. I'm going to try for catcher. I mean, if that's okay?"

"I don't believe it!" the coach exclaimed. "She hasn't played for two years, but runs like crazy. Hasn't hit for two years, but thinks she can bat .400. And," she added, throwing her hands into the air, "has never been a catcher but thinks she can be!" She swung toward Angie, who was standing closest to her. "I don't believe it! Do you?"

Angie smiled sweetly. "Oh, sure." She glanced around at the others and made a sweeping motion with her arm. "All the girls figure on Kelli's doing just that. No problem."

There was a murmur of agreement from the group.

The coach gave them all an odd stare. "Uh-huh." She started to walk away, signaling with her right arm as she did so. "Come on, we better go in before your brains all get more frozen than they already are. Next thing you'll be telling me you should be the favorites to win the conference because you've got her on your team." She continued walking, shaking her head as she went along.

The girls glanced at each other and then broke into peals of laughter.

Miss McGuire stopped and eyed them with a bemused look on her face. "I didn't mean it to be quite so funny," she finally said, as their laughter continued.

Now it was Sam's turn to respond. "Sorry, Coach. We aren't laughing at you. It's just that we were thinking the same thing ourselves. Guess it is sort of stupid, huh?" She winked at Kelli and laughed harder.

"Lord, help us," the coach said in a pleading voice, glancing heavenward as she spoke.

"He is, Coach," Kelli said softly. She draped one arm across Angie's shoulders and the other across Sam's. "Believe me, He already is."

CHAPTER FIVE

Eric

"OUR NAME DOESN'T MAKE ANY SENSE, YOU
know," Rayanne complained. "We should be named
something that goes with Fall River."

"Now what are you babbling about?" Darcy said
absently, unlacing her shoe and slipping it off. She
sighed contentedly as she rubbed her foot.

"Our name," Ray responded. "You know, the school's
nickname. Comets. What have comets got to do with
Fall River?"

"What do you want us to be called? The Fish?"

"Fall River Fish," Angie said, planting her right foot
on the locker bench and staring toward the ceiling.
"Yeah, I really like that. Has a nice ring to it, doesn't it?"

"I can hear the crowd screaming now," Sam joined in.
"Go fish, go fish! Swim on to victory, you fish!" She
made a motion with her mouth like a fish in water, and
the others collapsed into fits of laughter. "We could have

51

fins painted on our uniforms!"

"Well, I still don't understand about the name," Ray said when they had settled down. "Seriously, folks, does Comets really make sense?"

"Seriously, Ray, who really cares?" Darcy said as she stood in front of the mirror to put on fresh lipstick.

"Hey, did any of you see where those two people went—the ones I was talking to out there?" Kelli said. She walked over to the mirror and began brushing the snarls from her hair.

Mel shrugged. "Not me. Who were they, anyway? Your grandparents?"

"My grandparents! Come on! Did they look the same age? The lady's only about as old as my mother."

"Then who were they?"

"The man's my foster grandparent, and the lady runs the nursing home where he lives. I just met them yesterday."

"Foster grandparent? What in the world is that?" Several of the girls were paying attention now, waiting for Kelli to answer Mel's question.

"It's a program where a kid gets assigned an old person at the nursing home and then kind of adopts him or her as a grandparent. Angie and I are doing it through our church group, and I got Herman—that's his name." There were some snickers from the others, and she glared into the mirror in response. "Hey, don't knock it, okay? He's an all right guy—for an old man, I mean. He came all the way over here today to watch my opening practice, didn't he? Even gave me some advice before I went back up to the plate," she added half under her breath. "Wish he would've stuck around."

"Maybe he got too cold, or something," Sam interjected. "He looked pretty frail. He must be a hundred, huh?"

"Eighty-eight," Kelli replied. She finished brushing her hair, did a quick check on her makeup, and swung around to face the others. "Anybody for hitting Snyder's before we go home? I'm dying for a malt, and it's only five o'clock."

"Snyder's? You don't suppose Eric is working there today, do you?" Rayanne teased. She gave a little sigh and smiled sweetly in Kelli's direction.

"How would I know?" Kelli sniffed. But she was blushing just the same.

A week ago she had gone to a movie with Eric Walker, a good friend of her brother's. Eric and Tom had gone off to college together last year. Now it was the break between winter and spring terms, and Eric was home for a few days while Tom had taken off to visit a friend in Texas.

Going to the movie had been just a spur-of-the-moment thing, but now, as far as Kelli's crazy friends were concerned, Kelli and Eric were an "item." Still, Kelli had to admit that the thought of his working today at Snyder's had occurred to her before she made the suggestion to stop for a malt.

"Hey, Kelli! Quit dreaming and let's get going!" It was Angie at the locker room door.

Kelli glanced around. Everyone was gone except

Angie, who was impatiently holding the door. "This was your idea, you know?"

Kelli grabbed her purse and raced out the door. The weather had turned much colder; there was even a hint of snow in the air. The girls chattered noisily as they made their way in a group down the street from the school and onto Main Street where Snyder's was located.

"How's your brother doing, anyway?" Beth asked as they approached the cafe. "Does he like college yet?"

"Loves it. Says he's going to major in ergonomics."

"Ergo-what?" Sam asked.

"Ergonomics," Kelli answered. "The study of relationships between people and their work, I think."

"Ergonomics. Wow," Sam said. "I'd have to use my full name if I were going around telling people that I was in that. Here's my card," she said, pretending to hand Angie a business card. "As you can see, I'm an ergonomicist."

"I think it's ergonomist," Kelli said dryly.

"Right, ergonomist," Sam responded. She resumed her pose. "This is me, Samantha Ann Turner, ergonomist."

"Nice to meet you," Angie replied with a bow. "I'm Angie. Call me Ang."

"Knock it off!" Kelli exclaimed as they reached Snyder's doorway. "Eric's going to think we're all whacko."

Sam assumed her best "hurt" expression. "Oh, sure," she pouted. "Just when I start to learn a new word and act more mature, you come along and spoil it." She paused, then grinned slyly at the others. "I suppose I'll have to go back to being a high school girl, just because of dearest Eric." She put the back of her hand to her forehead and stared skyward. "Oh, the price of love." She dodged away from Kelli's attempt to give her a shove.

"Oh, hi, Eric," she said quickly as a tall, red-haired young man came from between two rows of greeting cards and nearly collided with her. "Say, how's your ergonomics?"

"Huh?" he said, giving her an odd stare. Kelli groaned softly, and the other girls giggled and hurried away.

"Hi," Kelli said shyly as Eric turned toward her.

"What's with her?" Eric asked.

"Oh, don't mind her," Kelli said. "We're all a little weird today. First day of softball practice, you know."

"Softball? I didn't think you played anymore."

"Well, I didn't. But everyone's talked me into trying again, so I'm giving it a shot. How're you doing?"

He smiled. "Great. Made a lot of money over break. Too bad it's over with day after tomorrow. I'll have to drive back on Sunday. How's Tom doing in Texas?"

"Fine, I guess. We've only talked to him once." Kelli stared down at her toes and began drawing a figure eight with her right foot. "Break's gone pretty fast, hasn't it?"

"Yeah," he agreed. "Especially for me with all this working." He waved his arms to indicate the store. "You got time to go out with me again before I leave?"

"Oh." She blushed. "Sure, I guess. Where to?"

"Another movie? My church has a good one tomorrow night."

"Your church?"

"Yeah. It's a story about a girl who is paralyzed and comes back to lead a successful life. I saw it at the campus chapel a couple weeks ago. What do you think?"

Kelli hesitated, then nodded. "Okay, but this isn't going to be something really heavy, is it? I'd like to be able to relax this weekend and not worry about the world's problems."

"It's not heavy. Actually, it's pretty inspiring. There's a book about her, too—it's a true story."

Kelli smiled. "Okay. What time?"

"About seven-thirty. The movie starts at eight."

"Great. See you then." She paused as she heard Sam and Angie laughing. "Right now, I think I'll go over and bash a couple of my friends."

Eric held out a roll of wrapping paper he had been carrying. "Here, use this and charge it to me."

It was seven-thirty when Kelli settled into her favorite chair with a bowl of popcorn and a copy of a new record magazine that had come in the mail. Just as she filled her mouth with a huge handful of popcorn, the phone rang.

"Ummph, great," she mumbled. "Never fails!" She hurried toward the insistent phone, chewing and swallowing as rapidly as possible on the way. Her cheeks still resembled a loaded down chipmunk's as she attempted to answer.

"Hi," she sputtered. "This is Kewwi."

"Kelli. Great! I was hoping you were home. This is Jared."

"Jawwod," she gulped quickly. "Jared! It's about time you got in touch with me. I suppose you've been hiding out, thinking I would try to get you, huh?"

"Now, why would I do a thing like that?" the youth group leader said with a laugh.

"You know why. First you 'volunteer' me, and then you give me an eighty-eight-year-old man! Some leader you are."

"It is amazing how good I am, isn't it?"

"Jared, it's lucky for you we're talking on the phone and not in person!" Kelli exclaimed.

"Kelli, Kelli, Kelli," he replied. "You know and I know you'll get along just great with old Mr. Hochman. In fact, that's why I'm calling. I was at the nursing home this afternoon, and Mrs. Horner said she had brought him over to watch your practice session today. Which reminds me . . . how did it go?"

"Well, just a few problems." She gulped. "Actually, Herman sort of helped me there, and then he just disappeared. It was pretty weird."

"He had a coughing spell, and Mrs. Horner rushed him right out of there. She was afraid it was getting too cold and he'd get really ill."

"I suppose I should go see him again."

"That's exactly why I was calling," Jared responded. "Mrs. Horner asked if I would get in touch with you. Herman asked if you could come by."

"Me? He asked for me?"

"By name. What do you think?"

"Yeah, sure." She twirled the phone cord around her arm and then stretched it out and sat down in a nearby chair. "Why do you think he wants to see me?"

"Why not? Don't you two get along?"

"I don't know. We've only met twice. I just wondered how come I got an old man, when there probably are a hundred old ladies in there who are just as alone as he is. Any special reason for putting me with him?"

Jared chuckled. "Ah, Miss Matthews, you are a suspicious soul. You think I had an ulterior motive?"

"Actually, I don't *think* so at all. Knowing you, I'm sure of it!"

"Okay, I confess," he laughed. "I asked that he be your assignment after I heard about his background."

"What's that supposed to mean?"

"Why don't you ask him yourself? That is, *if* you're going over to talk to him and keep him company for a while."

Kelli sighed. "I guess I am, aren't I? You don't think it's too late, do you?"

"Actually, no. They'll be glad to let you talk until eight-thirty, maybe even nine if you want. I asked."

"You're a bum, Jared, you know that. A bum."

"Why, Miss Matthews, such talk from someone so young. I hope you'll show more respect to Mr. Hochman." He chuckled again. " 'Bye."

Kelli quickly dumped the rest of the popcorn into a paper bag and hurried out to the second car. The bitter afternoon wind had died down, and now a star-filled, clear, crisp sky greeted her. She breathed deeply and then hopped into the car. Within minutes she was pulling into the visitor's spot near the front of the home.

No one was at the reception desk, so she walked quickly down the hall and stopped in front of Herman's door. Her heart felt like it had moved up into her throat, and it was pounding hard. She waited a few more seconds and then knocked. No response. Kelli stepped back, then reached forward and knocked again, harder this time.

"You don't need to break it down, you know."

Kelli jumped at the sound of the voice at her shoulder. She turned quickly and found the old man standing there with a slight grin on his face.

"Hold the noise down, will you? Don't you know this place is full of old people?"

"Sorry." Kelli laughed nervously. "You scared me half to death. I didn't hear you come up behind me."

"Course not. I was wearing these rubber-soled slippers." He pointed at his feet. "Darned comfortable, too, if I do say so myself. Well, since you're out here trying to bust down the door, you might as well come in." He pushed the door open and pointed inside.

Kelli eyed him suspiciously. "I thought you were sick in bed and asking for me. What're you doing out here wandering around the hall?"

"I live here, you know," he said indignantly. "I was out for my regular seven o'clock walk." He paused as if reflecting on that. "Except, of course, I ain't been taking the walk so regular the last few weeks while I was feeling poorly."

"What about your cough?"

"Ain't so bad. It just got to going there this afternoon, and I had a little trouble shuttin' it off, that's all. Really wasn't sick at all. In fact, I felt a darned sight better than I've felt in weeks. Did me a lot of good to get out into the fresh air. I wanted to come over and see if you had the gumption to get out there on the diamond. Glad to see you made it." He nodded toward her, a twinkle in his eye. "My advice worked, too, didn't it?"

He gave her a triumphant glance, and she nodded reluctantly.

"Thought so. Old lady Horner hustled me out of there so fast I didn't get to see you get all the way around the bases, but I figured it was all workin' out okay. I could hear the others cheerin' for you all the way over to the other side of the bleachers—even with the wind blowin' like it was." He nodded his head knowingly. "I could see what you were doin' out there—gettin' yourself all psyched out before you even tried. Now you got that outa your system, and you should be able to settle down and do some playin'. Right?"

"Yeah, sure. Right."

"Good. Now, we gonna stand out here in the hall jabbering all night, or do you have time to come in and sit down and talk like regular folks?"

She grinned. "Okay. Like regular folks." She started inside, then stopped again. "But how come you were asking for me? Jared—he's my youth leader over at church—Jared called and said Mrs. Horner said you were real sick and were asking for me."

Herman wrinkled his already wrinkled face even more. "Well, she just got things all confused. I was askin' for you, but I wasn't sick. Just coughin'. I was askin' for you because I wanted to talk with you about your baseball."

"Softball," she corrected.

He waved his hand impatiently. "Whatever. You play 'em all the same as far as I'm concerned." He shuffled in past her, walked over to a chair and sat down.

Kelli stood in the doorway a few seconds longer, then stepped across to the other chair and plopped down.

"So," they began together.

"Go ahead," she said, laughing self-consciously and nodding in deference to her senior host.

"Don't mind if I do." He settled back a bit in his chair. "I know I used to get real excited after the first day of practice. I felt that way again today out there watchin' you. Just thought we might chew the fat a bit about it—" he hesitated. "Uh, that is, if you don't mind?"

"No. I mean no, I don't mind. I was just surprised." She thought to herself how much more alert and active Herman had become since their first meeting.

"You're surprised?" he responded. "About what?"

"I don't know. That you found out about our practice and came over, and . . . and, well . . . you seem so different from before. What happened?"

"Nothing," he growled. "Just woke up again, that's all. After you came by, I got to thinking about all the days when I used to play. Got the old juices flowin' again." He stopped and coughed once. "Did I tell you I used to be pretty good?" He paused and nodded, speaking almost to himself, "Yep, pretty darn good." His voice broke slightly and he coughed again.

Kelli cleared her throat and forced a smile. "So, tell me about it. About your playing days, I mean."

"Not much to tell. I started playing in school. Liked it a lot and just kept on. Like I said, I played some in the outfield and did some pitching."

"You play in high school?"

He shook his head.

"How come?"

"Didn't have time to go to high school, that's why." His voice took on a slight edge, and his face flushed with anger. "My old man . . . my father, he came over from the old country. He thought school through grade eight was good enough. I could read and write, so why go on? Besides, he was trying to get his farming done, and he needed me and my brothers there. I tell you, farming, it wasn't easy back in them days. Did everything with horses, you know?" He sighed. "Yep, that was pretty much it for me with school, I guess."

"What about baseball?" Kelli demanded. "I thought you played when you were my age."

"I did, but no thanks to my dad. No sir . . . ma'am. He was dead set against it—both he and my mother. Baseball, well," he shook his head, "well, it took time out of the fields, and that was really a sin in their eyes. The farm was everything to my parents. Of course, now that I'm older I can see how good farming was for us. Back then I had problems with it. I really wanted to play baseball." He stopped and coughed loudly.

"So what did you do?" Kelli settled back further into her chair, trying to picture the time he was describing. "Did your mother and father finally let you play?"

"Nope. I had to do it on my own. We had a big argument about it, and finally I got them to agree I could play once a week with the town team. Well, we did pretty good, and the next thing you know one of them there scouts from the big leagues showed up one day. He watched me pitch a little, watched me hit some, said I was pretty good." He laughed. "I thought so, too, you know. Thought I was pretty hot stuff." He laughed again.

It was a warm, raspy laugh and it made Kelli laugh, too, in spite of herself.

"Well, anyway, after he watched us play, he came up and laid out this big legal-looking paper and asked if I wanted to sign. Told me I could play with the Cubs, up in the big leagues. But first I'd have to do some playing with one of them Triple A teams. Offered me a five thousand dollar bonus to sign and guaranteed another five thousand when I made it to the Cubs."

He stopped and glanced over at her. "That may not sound like much to you, but back in those days that was like about a million dollars to a farm kid like me. I figured I must've died and gone to heaven."

"Wow. So you went to one of those teams, then?"

"Nope. Never did. I figured if I was going to try baseball for money, I'd better get my ma and pa's blessing first. So, I went home and I told them all about it. They were excited about it, too, and that surprised me. Then Ma asked me one more question. 'Will it mean that you have to play on Sundays?' My ma, she was a strict one when it came to the Sabbath. Folks weren't as loose with their Sundays as they are today. No, sir. You kept the Lord's day for the Lord. Well, I thought about it for a bit, and I realized that I would have to play on Sundays—and it probably wouldn't just be with the Cubs. I'd probably have to play on Sundays with that Triple A team, too."

"So, your ma . . . uh, your mother, she wouldn't allow you to play?"

He laughed. "Wish it would've been that easy. Then I could have just been mad at her for a while. Nope, Ma, she did the tougher thing. She looked at me with her big, sad eyes and she said, 'Son, you can go ahead with this baseball thing if it means so much to you. But you know how I feel about the Sabbath. You give it some long, hard thought, then you do what you think is right.' Well, let me tell you, that was the longest, toughest night of thinking I've ever done. I had this little target built in the hayloft of our barn, and I used to go up there to practice my pitching. I went up there that night and I threw at that target until I thought I'd plumb near wore out my arm."

"Really?" Kelli was entranced.

He chuckled. "No, not really. Shucks, it would've took more than two or three hours of throwing to wear out my old arm. Anyway, I threw and threw, and then I picked up that ball and went down and told Ma I wouldn't be going with any Triple A team or with any Big League club. I'd stay home, play for the town team, and work the farm. I loved baseball," he said with a sigh. "But I loved my ma more. We always kept the Sabbath, and I still do." He sighed again and shook his head.

Kelli sighed, too. "Gee, I'm sorry that it never worked out for you, Mr. Hochman. I'll bet you would have been a great Major League player."

"Of course I would have," he said matter-of-factly. He looked over at her with a twinkle in his eye, watching to see her response. Then he roared with laughter. "Probably wouldn't have lasted a week with those big leaguers, and then I wouldn't have had a problem with the Sabbath anyway. And, I would've had that five thousand dollars to keep, no matter what. Oh, well. What would I have done with all that money, anyhow?"

CHAPTER SIX

Questions

KELLI TALKED WITH HERMAN HOCHMAN FOR ANother hour . . . one of the fastest hours of her life. He told her more about his town team, his family, and his life, and she sat soaking in every word.

"You have so much to talk about," she finally said with a sigh. "I wish I could stay longer, but I've got to get home and finish my homework. And we've got practice again tomorrow, too. I know I'll be stiff and sore in the morning; I can feel my muscles tightening up already."

"Well, you come to the right place for that, too, young lady," he said, getting up and hobbling over to his dresser. He rummaged through one of the bottom drawers and eventually pulled out a gray-green jar. "This here's muscle ointment. My pa's concoction. He passed it on to me, and I used it right up till I quit farming." He unscrewed the top, frowned, and then returned the lid. Walking back to where Kelli sat, he held it out to her. "This here's my secret weapon," he said. "Used it for baseball and after those long days in the field. Stuff's starting to dry out some, but you heat up the jar in some hot water, and then take it to your room before you open it up. Okay?"

"My room? Why?"

"Because that stuff smells like greased horses or worse." He chuckled as she wrinkled her nose in disgust. "Anyhow, just get this stuff softened up and smear it into your arms and legs and rub some on your neck and shoulders. Then bundle yourself up and get a good night's sleep. I guarantee you that in the morning you won't even know you had a workout today. But, you gotta get yourself up and going about a half hour earlier than usual."

"Why's that?" Kelli was puzzled.

"To soak in a tub full of bubble bath or something that smells decent, so you won't get tossed out on the street by your friends." His grin lit up the room. "That's the price you gotta pay. It's a half hour less sleep, but a week's worth less pain. Believe me."

Kelli didn't know why, but for some reason she did believe him, and it made her feel good inside that he cared enough about her to give her this jar of smelly ointment. She tucked the jar into her coat pocket and started for the door.

"And Kelli." His voice stopped her before she could turn the knob. "That swing you took today, that was just a starting point. It ain't gonna be so easy the next couple weeks. Takes gumption to go back after you get smacked in the head with a ball." Then he laughed lightly. "But I could see right off that you got plenty of that. Otherwise, why would you have bothered coming over to talk to an old goat like me in the first place!"

Kelli laughed, too, and went out into the crisp night air feeling better than she had felt in weeks.

Unfortunately, the feeling didn't last. She woke up with no aches and pains because, just as Mr. Hochman said, the ointment worked wonders. But all the ointment in the world couldn't get rid of the questions she had about herself and her ability to play softball again. She knew that in the next practice she'd have to stand in and take some swings with the bat. And, what was worse, she'd have to start catching again, taking throw after throw from the pitcher while someone stood directly in front of her swinging a bat. She broke out in a cold sweat just thinking about it—even while she was soaking in a warm bubble bath.

By the end of the school day Kelli's fear was multiplying, and she nearly jumped out of her skin when Angie tapped her on the shoulder as she stood near her locker after the final bell.

"Hey? You okay?"

Kelli nodded.

"You've hardly said two words all day. I thought maybe you were sick or something."

"No, nothing like that. Just a little nervous about practice."

"Why should you be nervous?" Angie asked. "You were great yesterday. Today will be a piece of cake."

"Maybe. I didn't have to stand bat yesterday. I just had to pretend."

As they jogged onto the practice field, Becky hurried over. "Your friend is here again." She gestured toward the first base line where Herman Hochman stood, leaning heavily on his cane. There was no one else around. He waved, and Kelli waved back.

"I'm going to talk to him for a minute." She ran across to where he was standing. "Hey, how'd you get over here?"

"I walked, of course. I got both my feet and this here cane. That gives me three to your two." He lifted the cane and pointed it at her legs.

"But you shouldn't be doing that, should you? I mean, all the way over from your place. That's about a mile."

"Only three-fourths. And it's about time I got out and did some walking. Can't do much of nothin' else, that's for sure." He paused and coughed. " 'Cept to cough, of course. I seem to get plenty of that done these days."

"Kelli! Let's go!" It was Coach McGuire. The rest of the team were already into warm-up drills.

"Look, you should take it easy. At least sit down and rest while you're here, okay?" She eased him toward the rickety bench which was used for the visiting team.

He smiled as she helped him sink down onto the bench, leaning heavily on his cane. "Good day for practice," he said, looking wistfully at the ball field. Then he reached over and patted her on the arm. "Thank you for your help. Now you get going or you'll be sitting on this bench with me—for the whole season!"

Kelli raced back to the warm-ups and was amazed at how good she felt. The rest of the girls were groaning and moaning as they tried to work the kinks out of their sore muscles. She grinned as she thought about how awful Mr. Hochman's horse grease smelled and how well it had worked. No one would believe her if she told them what she'd put on herself overnight.

"Okay," the coach said after they finished calisthenics and gathered around for the day's instructions. "I want five line drills across the infield, and then we'll work on our batting and fielding." She held out the catcher's mask. "Kelli, you might as well put this on and catch for me while I hit some fly balls to the outfielders and some grounders to the infielders. You can bat last." She nodded and tossed the face mask over to Kelli.

"Now, everyone on the first base line for a little friendly running!" They all groaned again, even Kelli this time, but at least half of her groan was at the thought of the softballs that soon would be flying toward her from all directions.

The running drills went quickly, and all too soon they were ready to start fielding. Coach McGuire sent the infielders over to one side to practice throwing grounders to each other and then motioned for the outfielders to go back for some fly balls. Nervously, Kelli slipped the mask into place and stood to one side of the coach.

"Okay," the coach said, "you all set?"

Kelli swallowed hard and nodded. The coach rocketed a long fly ball toward the outfield, and Kelli picked up another ball and tossed it to her. As the coach prepared to hit again, Darcy fielded the first ball and threw it toward Kelli. She watched it sail toward her, then at the last second she took several steps back and let the ball hit the ground and bounce. It rolled toward her, and she ran ahead as the coach hit again.

"Step ahead and catch those, don't back away from them!" Coach McGuire said sharply. "In a game situation, you're going to have to get to the ball and make the play."

Kelli nodded and pounded her glove as Angie caught the second hit ball and fired it toward them. Kelli ran forward to make the catch, then froze. She watched in horror as the ball came directly toward her head. "Kelli!" The sharp cry snapped her from her trance and she reacted fast, jerking the glove up and making the catch. She gulped and backed away as the coach smacked another ball toward the outfield.

"That's the kind of catching I want to see," the coach said with a nod. "Keep it going."

Kelli tossed her the ball and shook her head. "Thanks for yelling at me. It kept me from taking that one in the face."

The coach stopped in mid-swing. "I didn't yell at you," she said.

"No? I heard you yell Kelli."

Coach shook her head and chuckled. "Sorry, not me. You must have a guardian angel sitting on your shoulder." She hit another fly ball, while Kelli looked back toward the outfield for another throw.

"I know I heard somebody call my name," she muttered as she waited for the next throw. Over the next ten minutes, she caught ball after ball, feeling the old rhythm of catching and throwing start to return. After the fly-ball drill, the coach began batting grounders to the infield. These throws came in sharper and straighter, and Kelli felt her confidence grow as she handled each one better than the one before.

"Okay," the coach said. "Let's see how we can hit." She blew her whistle and signaled for the team members to gather around. "Kelli, you might as well get the catching gear on, and we'll do this right. I'll pitch and you catch, and we'll see how everyone can handle the bat. Lara can do some catching, too, so you'll get your chance to bat."

Kelli picked up the leg guards and chest protector and moved over to where Herman Hochman sat leaning forward on his cane.

"Not too bad out there, young lady," he said, still keeping his gaze straight ahead. "Just about got yourself beaned though. Glad you heard me holler."

Kelli stopped strapping on one of her leg guards. "You're the one who yelled? How'd you know I was having trouble? I was turned away from you."

"I didn't need to see your face to see you weren't ready to catch," he answered. "The ball was coming in and you still had your arms at your sides." He turned toward her. "I just didn't want you gettin' hurt."

A warm feeling washed over Kelli, and she smiled an

embarrassed smile. Mr. Hochman nodded at her and then turned back to face the field.

Coach McGuire waited until Kelli came over and then had everyone sit down while she talked: "I want you each to play your normal positions, and we'll let everyone take a few cuts with the bat to see what you can do. Lara, you be the first batter, and then I want you to replace each of the other girls as they come in for a turn. I'll do all the pitching today, so Kari and Becky, you just take some turns batting and then I want you to go over to the bullpen and work on pitching to each other."

She paused and pulled out her clipboard. "Okay, we'll have Kari bat first, then Becky, then Lara. Then we'll start the rotation. All four infielders, then the three outfielders, and Kelli last. You guys looked pretty good on handling the ball, and it's going to pay off to play good defense. But we've got to hit the ball and score some runs, too, and this is the place to start."

She clapped her hands, and the girls jumped up and raced to their spots. Kelli stepped in behind home plate and put one knee down. The coach walked out to the pitching rubber and turned to face her. "I'll throw you a couple and then we'll get started," she called.

Kelli nodded.

The coach set with both hands in front of her, then windmilled her arm back and launched the ball toward home. Kelli gritted her teeth and made the catch. The ball made a satisfying "thwack" as it settled into her glove. She threw it back without standing and glanced over toward Herman. He was still leaning forward on the cane and looking out toward the pitcher's mound. After two more tosses, Kari stood in and took a practice swing.

Kelli warily eyed the bat swinging before her eyes as she leaned back on her right knee. The coach checked on each of her fielders, then windmilled in the pitch. Kelli watched the ball and out of the corner of her eye saw Kari tighten up to swing. Beads of sweat popped out on her forehead, and she felt her throat go dry. Her vision started blurring, and she pulled her glove up to protect her face. Kari swung and missed, and the ball hit the corner of Kelli's glove and skidded off wildly toward the bench where Herman was sitting. He leaned down and picked it up as Kelli trotted over to retrieve it.

"What do you call that?" he asked sharply.

"Huh?" Kelli stopped, surprised at his tone.

"You call that catching? My mother could catch better than that."

"Hey, who do you think you are?" Kelli asked angrily.

"I'm an old man who hasn't played any ball for a long time, but I think I could do better than you just did. If you're going to sit back there and protect your face just because you once got hit in the head, then you might as well quit and go on home. You told me you wanted to be a ball player again. Well, then you better keep your eyes on the ball and try to catch it."

Kelly grabbed the ball from his hand. "I didn't just get 'hit in the head,' " she exclaimed. "I got bashed in the head and broke half the bones in my face and couldn't see straight for a whole year. No, I don't want to get hit

74

again. I'm scared!"

"Every ball player gets scared sometimes," he said quietly. "You have to put that behind you and try again. If you start thinking that every pitch is going to hit you—whether you're catching or hitting—then you'll never do anything to help your team. You've got to block it out of your mind and start again. Being scared is okay, because it's going to make you more alert. Be scared, but don't let it stop you from being the player I know you can be. I know you can be good—" he stopped and shook his head and looked directly into her eyes. "I know you can be great if you try."

Coach McGuire walked over to where they were glaring at each other. "What's going on?"

"Nothing," Kelli said. "I'm just explaining to Mr. Hochman why I didn't catch that ball."

"And I was telling her why she won't have to miss any more," he said with a gruff smile. He held out his hand to the coach. "I'm Herman Hochman, and I think this young lady's going to be a very fine ball player. If you don't mind, I'm planning to sit here for a while and try to make sure she doesn't give up on herself."

The coach looked from one to the other and then took the ball out of Kelli's hand. "No problem, but let's get on with it. I've got ten other girls out here who plan to be fine ball players, too, you know." She reached over and shook Herman's hand and then wheeled about and headed for the pitcher's rubber. "You going to catch or should I put Lara in?" she called over her shoulder.

Kelli toed the ground for a second. "I'm catching," she

said. She took a step toward home plate, then stopped and looked back. "What makes you an expert on this, anyway?" she asked. "You always did great. You never had to try to start over like I'm trying to do."

The old man slowly reached up and pulled back the hair on the left side of his head, revealing an angry purple scar about three inches long. "That took twenty-five stitches and two days in the hospital. I was out cold for more'n two hours." He let the hair drop back down and motioned toward the plate. "Now, go on back and do it right."

His face contorted and he began to cough. He coughed harder and harder, then slipped from the bench onto the ground.

"Coach!" Kelli screamed, rushing to his side. "Quick. Help!"

Coach McGuire dropped the bat she was holding and raced across the infield toward them. As she ran off the field she stepped into a hole. Even from where she stood, Kelli could hear the snapping sound as the coach fell and rolled. "My leg!" the coach yelled.

"Angie! Help her!" Kelli hollered. She looked from Coach McGuire to Herman, both lying on the ground. "God help me," she prayed aloud. "What should I do?" She took a deep breath.

Angie and Mel raced toward their fallen coach, and Kari hurried over to where Kelli was kneeling by Mr. Hochman's side.

Stay calm, stay calm.

Kari reached her.

"Get to the gym and call nine-one-one," Kelli said as she leaned over and lifted the old man's head onto her knee. "Tell them we need two ambulances, right away!"

CHAPTER SEVEN

Guardian Angel

"THAT WAS SCARY!" SAM SAID AS SHE WRAPPED A towel around her wet hair and flopped down on the locker room bench next to Kelli. "What did the paramedics say?"

"Coach broke her ankle for sure . . . pretty bad, too." Kelli gulped hard. "I don't know about Mr. Hochman, but he looked pretty pale when they put him into the ambulance. I should've gone with him to the hospital."

"No, you shouldn't have," Angie said, sitting down on the other side of her friend and putting an arm around her. "We were all screaming and yelling at you to come over and help us with Coach, and you know it."

"You can't blame yourself for what happened to him, you know," Mel said. "What did that old dude say to you, anyway, that got both of you so agitated?"

"Agitated," Beth said with a whistle as she yanked open her locker door and pulled out her letter jacket.

"Wow, listen to who's using big words now."

"He's not an 'old dude,' " Kelli protested. "His name is Mr. Hochman, and he didn't say anything wrong. It was me who was out of line, and that's what got him started coughing so hard." Tears started streaming down her face. "Now he's in the hospital and who knows how bad off he is, and the coach has a broken ankle, and everything's my fault." She buried her face in her hands.

"Hey," Mel said, putting a comforting hand on Kelli's shoulder. "I'm sorry I called him an old dude. But you shouldn't be blaming yourself, Kelli. You said he shouldn't have been out there in the first place, and you're probably right. The way the wind was whipping around, it even made some of us start coughing. He should've known better than to be sitting out there in this weather."

Kelli wiped at her eyes, then got up and put on her coat without speaking. She started toward the door.

"Look, you don't have to be mad at your friends just because you think you're to blame for what happened to Mr. Hochman," Angie said, hurrying to Kelli's side.

"Oh, Ang, I'm not," Kelli said tearfully. "I just don't want him to die or something because he came out there to keep me from playing poorly. I don't know what it is about him, but almost since the minute I met him, he's been doing his best to keep me from quitting the team. Today, I got mad at him for trying to help me, and now he ends up in the hospital. I don't want him to get sick or die because of me."

"Well, if he's the one who got you around those bases so fast yesterday, then I'm going to say a strong prayer for his recovery," Angie said.

"That goes for me, too," Ray said from the corner.

"That goes for all of us," Darcy added.

"I think we ought to say a prayer right now for your Mr. Hochman," declared Becky. The room grew quiet.

"And for Coach McGuire, too," Sam said.

They all nodded and stood, gathering around Kelli as if looking to her for leadership. She held out her hand to Angie, and the girls all clasped hands and bowed their heads while Kelli prayed for the speedy recovery of the two adults.

"There," Angie said with a bright smile as they looked up. "Now quit feeling sorry for yourself and be thankful he came to help you out. Okay?"

Kelli glanced around at her teammates and nodded. Inside, though, she still felt sick about what had happened, and as she left the gym, her tears returned. She ran all the way home, bursting into the kitchen and hurrying past her startled mother to her room. Throwing herself on the bed, she sobbed quietly until a soft knock interrupted her. "Go away," she sniffed.

"Kelli, we need to talk." Her mother's voice was muffled through the door. "I'm coming in."

Kelli heard the door open and then felt her mother's gentle touch on her shoulder. "Oh, Mom," she cried, turning her face against her mother as she felt the comforting arms wrap around her.

"Kelli, I heard what happened at the field today.

Everything's okay."

"But, Mom, Mr. Hochman looked so bad. He . . . he. . . ."

"He's going to be fine. A woman called a little while ago from the home, and he's there resting. He asked if you can come by to see him first thing tomorrow. Your coach called, too. She's a little worse off and has to stay in the hospital a few days. She wants you to come and see her tomorrow afternoon." Her mother leaned back. "Now, if I were you, I'd dry those eyes and come on down to eat something."

"I just want to lie here a while, Mom. Okay?"

"Okay," her mother said with a sigh. "But if I were you, I'd want to get a bite to eat before getting ready for my date."

Kelli sat bolt upright. "Eric! Oh my gosh, I forgot about our date!" She glanced at the clock. "Six forty-five! Mom!"

"I suppose it has to be Supermom to the rescue once again. I do get tired of pulling off one miracle after another."

"Please, Mom, don't take tonight off," Kelli implored her mother as she began racing around the room. She stopped and glared at herself in her dresser mirror and then threw up her hands. "So far this day's been a total disaster, and I don't want my date with Eric to be one, too."

"Eric already knows all about Mr. Hochman, because I told him," Mom said. "If he's the thoughtful young man I think he is, he'll be very understanding about your not having time to get ready. Beside, you are a very pretty young woman, and any young man would be proud to be seen with you."

Kelli hurried to give her mother a big hug.

"Thanks, Mom. You really are a super mom, you know?"

"I do my best," her mother agreed, holding her daughter out at arm's length to look her over. "But I'm not a fairy godmother, so I'd recommend that even if you don't have time to change your clothes, you still take a minute or two to comb your hair. I don't have a magic wand to do the trick."

"Maybe not," Kelli said as she gave her mom another big hug, "but you're a magic person in every other way, and I love you!"

The movie was warm, wonderful, sad, and inspiring, all rolled into one, and Kelli and Eric were still talking about it an hour after it ended. They sat together at McDonald's, sharing a bag of french fries and sipping on soft drinks.

"It's too bad we can't all be as courageous as that girl," Kelli sighed.

"Sometimes I think we are," Eric answered. "Oh, don't get me wrong," he said quickly as Kelli registered an expression of dismay, "we're not nearly as heroic as she is, but people show a lot of courage in making day-to-day decisions, too, you know. Just look at you. You decided to go back out for softball, even though it scares you half to death. I'm sure we all have things like that happening all the time. It takes courage to make the right choices."

"Well, maybe."

"Hey, and look at me," he exclaimed. "I had to get up the courage to ask you out tonight even though I should be studying and getting ready for school."

Kelli burst into laughter at his sudden confession. "Okay. I'm glad you had the courage to ask me out. But, what you should really get is a medal for being seen with me, the way I look. I came home from practice feeling and looking pretty pathetic, and I barely got ready before you arrived."

She held out her hands to him, and he took them with a smile. "If you look bad, then I'd like to see what someone who looks good looks like."

Kelli blushed and glanced around to see if anyone was watching them. Across the room she saw Sam's head disappear behind the top of a booth. "Oh, brother," she muttered, "now I'll have to put up with her for the next week."

"What?" Eric responded.

Kelli jerked a thumb in Sam's direction, and Eric glanced over just in time to see Sam peek up over the top of the booth, this time joined by Ray and Krissie. He grinned at them and waggled his fingers in greeting. The trio ducked down again and Kelli could hear them giggling, even above the other noise in the place.

"Your friend Sam is weird sometimes, you know that?"

"You should see her out on the ball field. She gets

absolutely loony during some practices."

Eric's face sobered. "Say, I heard about old Mr. Hochman. Is he going to be all right?"

"Yeah, I guess," she said, forgetting about her friends and concentrating on her conversation. "I'm going over to see him tomorrow. I can't figure him out. He's only known me for a few days, and he acts like he's my—" she paused, trying to think of a descriptive word. "How about grandfather?"

Eric said. "Or father? Or hey, maybe he's trying to be your coach."

"Maybe. Or maybe something more. It's almost like . . . like he's me. Does that make any sense? Everything I do out on the ball field, he's doing it with me, at least in his head. He sits there and watches what I'm doing, and then he chews me out when I don't do something the way he thinks it should be done. It's like he's trying to make up for some mistakes he made by making sure I don't make them, too."

"Doesn't sound too bad to me," Eric said, leaning back with a slight smile on his face. "Sounds like you've got yourself your very own guardian angel. You should be happy."

"But who does he think he is, anyway?"

Eric held up both hands in self-defense. "Hey, if the old fellow feels good by helping you out and keeps you out of trouble by doing it, why get upset? He's only watching over you at the ball field, right?"

She nodded.

"So, it's no big deal. It's not like he's with you twenty-four hours a day."

She pondered that for a few seconds before nodding. "Yeah, I suppose. I'm just not sure whether I should be pleased or mad. I'm glad he wants me to do well, but at the same time it's embarrassing having him sit there and point out all the things I'm doing wrong."

"Tell him that," Eric said with a shrug. "If it were me, that's what I'd do. He could watch me all he wanted and then tell me later what I was doing right or wrong. It's like when your mom or dad come to watch you, right? You're glad they're there, but you don't want them to say anything in front of your friends."

Kelli grinned. "That's exactly right."

Eric leaned back and cupped his chin in his hand. "I didn't realize I'd learned so much in Psych 101. I should be charging for all this great advice. I hear psychologists make about a hundred dollars an hour."

Both Eric and Kelli jumped when a face suddenly appeared at the window beside them. Sam put her nose against the window and smiled sweetly before waving a little baby wave to each of them. "Bye, bye," she said loud enough for them to hear her through the window. "Have fun, but not too much fun, if you know what I mean."

"I can hear it now," Kelli said with a sigh. "By Monday afternoon everyone in the high school will think you and I are going steady. Tell you what, Dr. Walker. You give me some advice on how to take care of Sam, and I'll gladly pay you a hundred dollars an hour." They laughed together and waved at Sam and the other girls as they piled into Sam's car and drove away.

"Send your guardian angel after her," Eric said as he turned back toward her.

"He's not my—" Kelli stopped in mid-sentence as she noticed the twinkle in Eric's eye. "Sorry," she said. "I guess I shouldn't get so upset about Sam, or about Mr. Hochman."

"You're right, you shouldn't. As for Sam, I hope she *does* tell everyone that you and I are more than just friends, because I'd like it to be true."

"Really?"

"Really."

Kelli blushed again. "Me, too."

She reached over and took his hands again, feeling a warm glow spread through her as she did so. At the same time, she thought again about Herman Hochman and Eric's remark.

"That's it!" she exclaimed, pulling her hands away. "With Coach out, it's perfect. Why didn't I think of it before?"

"What?" he asked. "What are you talking about?"

"Guardian angels! I mean, coaches." She stopped and giggled. "Mr. Hochman and Sam. Maybe I *should* send him after her. Maybe I should have him go after the whole team."

"What are you talking about?"

"Oh, Eric!" she said, jumping up and moving over beside him. "What a great idea!" She gave him a big hug, and Eric stared at her with a shocked expression while people in nearby booths nodded toward them and smiled. "Come on, let's go back to my place. I've got to tell Mom and Dad!"

She started toward the door, dragging him by the hand, but he pulled to a stop.

"Would you mind letting me in on it first?"

"Don't you see?" she said excitedly. "Mr. Hochman doesn't have to be just *my* guardian angel. He can help all of us. With his skills and knowledge, he can coach us while our real coach recovers. This is going to be fantastic!"

"What's wrong with your coach?" Eric asked. "I haven't heard about this."

"Oh, it's a long story. I'll tell you on the way. Come on!"

Eric exchanged a weak smile and shrug with three women sitting in a booth by the door. "This is a fantastic idea," he told them, "and I'm the one who thought of it . . . I think."

CHAPTER EIGHT

Kelli's Solution

"But Mr. Hochman knows everything there is to know about the game!"

"I'm sure he does," Coach McGuire said, "but why does that mean that I have to rely on him to take over until I can get back with the team? I think I ought to hire someone from the college who knows something about teaching."

"No! I mean, couldn't you consider him a special assistant or something? He's got something special going for him, and I just know that if we put him in there it'll all work out for the best. He's like a . . . well . . ." Kelli paused. "You'd laugh if I told you what I really think."

"Try me."

"Guardian angel," Kelli said weakly.

Her coach's jaw dropped. "A what?"

"Well, not really, but that's the best I can do, because that's about what he's been for me ever since I met him—at least as far as softball is concerned." She hurried on before her coach could interrupt.

"I've prayed and prayed about this, and I think it's something that was meant to be. I mean, why would I have to make the decision on whether or not to come out for softball and then, almost at the same time, meet Mr. Hochman? I've been worried since the first minute about how I'd do on the team, and every step of the way Mr. Hochman has been there to make sure I keep moving ahead. And that's not all. He was there for me, but I was there for him, too. I met him when he was really down, and now he has something good to work for, to live for."

"So God's part of this, too, huh?" Coach asked. "How did He get involved?"

"Through my church youth group. At least, that's how I got hooked up with Mr. Hochman. Oh, it's a long story. But the point is, I'm sure that God meant for us to meet. Ever since I met him and he met me, we've both been doing a lot, lot better."

"Oh, sure. I saw how much better he was doing when they carted him off in the ambulance yesterday," Coach McGuire said sarcastically. She gestured toward her upraised leg. "Just before they loaded me into the next one, which, by the way, was probably his fault, too."

"Coach, that was a hole you fell in. You can't blame that on Herman, even if you were running over to help him."

Coach sighed. "You're right. I should have seen the hole. But that doesn't mean I shouldn't be worried about putting an old man in charge of my team—especially an old man who collapsed after walking to practice."

"Well, that was yesterday, and he wasn't nearly as bad off as we all thought. When I talked to him this morning, the first thing he asked me was whether or not I went back out and caught the ball the way I should have. Now, the next thing I have to do is work on my batting. With him out there, I know I can make it."

Kelli paced nervously over to the window and glanced outside, then whirled back toward her new coach. "Listen, you don't know everything about me and why I haven't been out for softball for the past couple of years." She waved her hands as the coach started to say something. "But it doesn't matter. I'm back out, and I think I can help the team. Except . . . except I've got a couple of problems to work out yet, and if Mr. Hochman is there, I know I can do it."

Coach McGuire gestured for Kelli to come over to her bedside and pointed at the chair. When Kelli was seated, she looked her straight in the eye. "Kelli, I don't know. . . ."

"Please, please," Kelli begged. "Trust me. I know this is what God wants us to do."

Coach smiled and nodded. "If you're that sure, who am I to say no? Besides, if you really do have God on your side, this team's going right to the state tournament, because I don't know of any other teams with that kind of support."

"Thanks. Oh, thanks!" Kelli leaned forward and

hugged her coach hard. "Now I've got to get this schedule over to Marilyn Horner at the nursing home. She's already got the car lined up to bring Herman, and—" she stopped in mid-sentence at the look on Coach's face. "What?"

"You already had someone lined up to bring that old man out to practice, even though I hadn't approved it?"

"Well, you see. . . ."

"I hope you're half as confident about how well our team is going to do this year!" The coach burst into laughter. "I'll have to get acquainted with this guardian angel," she said. "After I get back on my feet, I figure I'll win 'Coach of the Year' for leading this team to the state championship because of his great assistance! I'll want to know whom to thank."

"We can all thank God!" Kelli shouted as she hurried out the door, leaving the coach shaking her head in disbelief.

"Hmmph," Herman half-snorted.

"Don't get huffy about it. You know you could help out the team. Look what you did for me in only two days. Even if you only saw one thing wrong each day, it would really help. Mr. Hochman," Kelli pleaded, "even if you're just there for me, it will be terrific. I need you."

Herman looked away toward the window and brushed at his eyes. He was seated in the chair near his television set, a spot he had held since Kelli's arrival more than half an hour earlier. Now, after listening to

91

her plan, he had started to argue against it.

"Young lady," he said gruffly as he turned back, his eyes slightly moist. "I'm glad you think I can help you, but I'm an old man. I don't get around like I used to. Look what happened to me yesterday. Why, I'll be lucky to walk back and forth on the field to explain what you're doing wrong."

"Then stay in one spot and tell us. We'll listen to you, I'll guarantee it. I talked to Marilyn, and she said she'd ask the country club to loan us a golf cart. You can use that to go back and forth and coach us."

She sat back on his bed and glared at him. "Now stop making excuses. You're not too old!"

"Hmmph. I don't like the tone of your voice. Didn't your parents ever teach you to respect your elders?"

Kelli gasped. "Oh, I'm sorry. I didn't mean to be rude."

He chuckled. "I guess it is about time I got up and out of this here chair and started doing something useful."

"Oh," she squealed, jumping up and hugging him.

"But not if you squeeze me half to death before I even get started," he growled. "I ain't made of stone, you know." He pointed toward his shoulder. "These old bones are getting a mite brittle. No need to put me up in the hospital before I even get a chance to show you what a great coach I am!"

Kelli stepped back quickly, a worried frown crossing her face. Then Herman grinned and gave her a high five.

"We start Monday," she said. "It'll be the same time as on Friday, so you better have Marilyn bring you over around three o'clock. Coach McGuire said it will probably be at least a week before she's able to even stand on the sidelines on crutches. Our first game is in twelve days, so until then, it's going to be up to you."

"Phewie," he exhaled with a slight whistle. "The last time anybody said that to me was when my old man got sick and I had to take over the farm for the summer. Let me tell you, I hope this here goes a little better than that."

"What happened?"

"We darned near lost the place, that's what happened."

"You did? How?"

"Well, actually, it was pretty easy. You see, it was 1933, and we got hit with the Dust Bowl and the Great Depression all rolled into one. You ain't going to have any calamities like that now, are you?"

She laughed. "Wow, I hope not. All you have to worry about is taking care of eleven teenaged girls."

Mr. Hochman whistled again and leaned back. "Now that you put it that way, this job's going to be a lot tougher than I thought!"

CHAPTER NINE

Filling In

"PARNELLI KINSEY, RACE CAR DRIVER SUPREME, TO the rescue!" Jared wheeled the golf cart sharply around the corner of the backstop as he yelled the greeting, then pulled it to a screeching stop in front of the diamond, where the softball team were going through stretching exercises. "Now, where's my man Herman? Let's get this show on the road!"

"Jared? What in the world are you doing here?" Angie stepped up and touched the side of the cart.

Jared sat behind the steering wheel with his knees nearly touching his chin. "What kind of welcome is that? I take a special vacation just so I can come out here and drive your new coach around, and that's the greeting I get." He hung his head. "I'm hurt."

"Oh, come off it," Kelli grinned. "Are you serious?"

"As God is my witness," he replied, holding his chin up and placing his right hand over his heart. "Now where's Mr. Hochman? Marilyn Horner said he might need an A-one chauffeur, and that's me if I ever heard of one. Nothing but the best for my favorite girls' softball team in all of Fall River."

"We're the only girls' softball team in all of Fall River," Krissie said.

"That makes it much easier for fans like me," he said. "Now, where's my passenger?"

"I think that must be him coming," Rayanne said, pointing toward a car pulling in near the bleachers. They all turned to look as the car stopped and Marilyn Horner got out and hurried around to the passenger side. A gasp rippled through the group as the old man stepped from the car.

Sam emitted a low whistle. "Would you look at that," she said softly. "Where did that old du—"she stopped, glanced at Kelli, and blushed. "I mean, where did he ever find that?"

The old man started toward them, walking stiffly but looking taller than Kelli remembered him. He was wearing a beautiful cardinal red jacket with a streak of yellow-gold across the center. Emblazoned above the streak was the word "Comets," also in yellow-gold letters. A ring of yellow-gold circled each sleeve at the point where the sleeve met the shoulder. He wore a cardinal red cap with a large yellow-gold "C" in the front. Sam whistled again, this time louder, as Herman strode up to them and stopped as if waiting for a response to his appearance.

Marilyn walked over to join them, smiling.

"You look great!" Sam exclaimed. "What a terrific jacket. Where did you get it? That is absolutely fabulous!"

"Come on, Sam," Beth said dryly, "just spit it out. Do you like the jacket or don't you?" All the girls laughed and moved forward to admire it.

"Hey! Hey!" Kelli jumped ahead of them and waved her arms. "Hold it, will you? This man is going to be our coach, and I don't think he wants to be crushed to death on his first day." The other girls nodded and stepped back.

Herman frowned. "I don't think they would've hurt me none, but I'm glad for your concern," he said. "I'm also glad you all like my old uniform jacket." He touched it lovingly. "Now we got some work to do." He turned and nodded to Marilyn, who gave him a little wave and walked away. Then he signaled to Jared, and the gangly young man stepped forward. "You know how to drive that thing?" He pointed toward the golf cart.

"Like a pro," Jared said. "Just ask the girls."

They all began booing in response, and he shrugged.

"Well, I'll be driving it like a pro soon, you just wait and see."

"Okay," Herman said, reaching out and taking Jared's hand. "My life is in your hands."

The girls laughed, and Jared chuckled.

"Now, young ladies, my name is Herman Hochman, but I'm sure Kelli's already told you all about me." He glanced over at her as he spoke. "I've never done any coaching before, but Kelli seems to think I've got a thing or two to share that might be of some help to you as you get ready to start your season. Now," he glanced around at them, "I'm sorry about what happened to your coach, and I don't mind telling you that I feel a little responsible for that. So I guess the least I can do is try to share some of the things I know about this game and hope that makes up a bit for her being gone."

He walked stiffly over to the home plate, picked up a bat, and then settled into the passenger side of the cart. He raised the bat with one hand. "One way to win some games is to use this thing to drive in some runs." Then he pointed it toward the center field fence. "Running the bases is another way, and you have to be in good shape to do that. You sprint out and back to that fence twice; then jog it once; then sprint it once more." He leaned back and planted the bat on the ground in front of him. "When you're done, we'll see how good you can handle one of these."

The girls glanced at one another, not sure how to react to his orders.

"Well, what're we waiting for?" Angie said. "If we're going to be Comets, we'd better fly." She took off for the fence, and with a yell the others followed. Kelli held back for a split second, gave two "thumbs up" signals to Herman and Jared, and then raced to catch her teammates as they sprinted toward the center field fence.

"What a slave driver," Darcy moaned.

"Without a doubt," Beth replied. "Kelli, we should throw you into Fall River for doing this to us."

From the spot where she lay sprawled on the locker room bench, Kelli half-laughed and half-groaned in response. "Good idea," she finally said. "That way, I'll at least be out of my misery."

"Was it my imagination, or was he even harder on you than on us?" Sam asked as she slowly leaned back against her locker.

"I don't know. Was he?"

"Yeah," Sam answered. "He definitely was. But, whatever he was saying to you about hitting and catching, it sure worked. Your catching was terrific, and you were swinging the bat almost as well as you did before—" she stopped. "Well, anyway, you looked really good."

"Sam's right," Angie added, her spiked shoes clattering on the concrete floor as she walked to the sink. "Mr. Hochman may be coming down on you, Kelli, but it's working. I wish he'd say something to me." She turned to the mirror and splashed some water on her face.

Kelli thought about the scene on the field. With Herman looking on, she had stepped in to bat for the first time, then quickly backed away as Kari had wound up and thrown in the pitch.

"Hey! What're you doing?"

"I—I don't know," Kelli answered as the old man walked over behind her and the ball came neatly across the plate into Lara's catcher's mitt. "I was afraid," she said softly, glancing toward the ball and swallowing hard.

"Well, ya can't be," he said gruffly. "Ya gotta stand in and ya gotta swing. If you don't do it now, you never will." He half-yanked the bat from her hands and pointed toward the plate. "I'm probably a pretty worthless old coot by now, but even as poor as I'm feeling and looking, I wouldn't be afraid to stand in there and swing the bat at the ball. Now, you've shown me more gumption and ability than that, and I ain't going to let you quit." He glared at her. "You ain't a quitter, are ya?"

Kelli's face turned red and she grabbed the bat back.

"Good," he said, taking a couple steps back. "Now, swing it at that ball like you're takin' a swing at me, and you'll be the best dang hitter in three counties."

Kelli gritted her teeth, stepped in, eyed the ball, and banged out a solid line drive to left field. "How's that?" she exclaimed, anger in her tone.

"What?" Angie's question brought her back out of her thoughts and into the locker room.

"Oh! I'm sorry," Kelli said, realizing she had spoken the last words out loud. "What did you just say to me?"

"I asked if you thought I batted awful."

"No. No, not that bad."

"Well, I did," Angie answered. "I was terrible today."

"Yeah, me too," Kari said as she began unlacing her shoes. "The only thing is, I'm the pitcher, so I don't have to be such a great hitter. I can save you all with my pitching."

The others groaned and pelted her with dirty socks.

"We all have to work on our hitting," Sam said seriously. "Besides Kelli, and Krissie of course, we all looked pretty bad." She raised her voice. "Krissie, do you ever have a bad day batting? You always look great."

Krissie shrugged. "It was just easy for me today," she said. "Easy pitches for me to hit."

"Hey, I was pitching, and I wasn't easing up on you," Kari said.

"Uh oh," Kris said with a frown. "You mean those were your best pitches? We're in trouble."

Her teammates laughed, and Kari put her thumb on the faucet and sprayed water in Krissie's direction.

"You're in for it now," Kris said, racing to the other faucet and spraying water back.

"Water fight!" Angie yelled, grabbing a water bottle from the shelf and splashing the rest of its contents over Sam's head. Sam shrieked and grabbed another bottle as Kris and Kari continued their battle. Angie tossed the empty bottle to Rayanne, who quickly began filling it at a third sink.

"Prepare to be melted," Sam said, taking the top off the bottle and advancing menacingly toward Angie.

"No, no," Angie giggled, backing toward the doorway. "Ray, help! Get her."

Sam glanced out of the corner of her eye toward Rayanne, and Angie took advantage of the moment to grab the handle of the door. "Oh, no, you don't!" Sam cried. She pulled back the bottle and sloshed it toward Angie just as Angie yanked open the door and nearly ran head-on into Mr. Hochman. The water splashed over both of them, and the yelling and shrieking came to a halt as the girls gasped in unison.

"Uh, hi," Angie said meekly as water dripped off her head and ran from Herman's face. Kelli buried her face in her hands to stop from laughing while the other girls, soaked from their brief water fight, looked fearfully at one another.

Angie stepped back from the door, picked up her towel and gingerly handed it to their new coach. He took it, wiped his face and handed it back, his face a stern mask.

"I was just going to come and see if everyone was doing okay," he began. "Some of you looked a little stiff and sore after practice." He looked around the room. "But, I can see you're all doing just fine, so tomorrow we'll add a couple more drills to our practice session." He started to leave, then turned back. "Oh, and if I were you, I'd mop up this mess before anyone leaves tonight, because I'm planning to come back in an hour and check it. If it ain't cleaned up, you'll all run a couple of extra wind sprints at the end of tomorrow's practice."

Then he smiled. "You know, I think I'm going to like coaching a lot more than I expected."

Over the next two days, Herman seemed to be everywhere—at least that's the impression he made on Kelli and her teammates. With Jared driving the golf cart, he went quickly from one part of the ball field to another. One minute he was yelling at Beth and Darcy for not concentrating hard enough on catching fly balls in the outfield, then within seconds, it seemed, he was at Sam's side over at first base, working with her on stretching and reaching for her teammates' throws rather than waiting for the ball to arrive. Then he was back to the outfield, patting Beth and Darcy on the back for "doing a great job in catching the ball the way he wanted it caught!"

When Becky was pitching, he was both encouraging and correcting, peering past her shoulder as she went into her windup, then offering advice on how to make her pitching moves more deceptive. Three pitches later, when Becky made a perfect toss and had her fellow pitcher Kari swinging wildly, Herman gave her his gruff approval. Then he had Jared chauffeur him quickly to the plate. "Make that a level swing, young lady," he growled. "You swing the bat correctly and you'll hit the ball."

A few seconds later he grunted his approval and Jared chuckled his appreciation as Kari's straight, smooth swing propelled Becky's pitch into right field for a base hit. "See!" he exclaimed. "Level swing."

Running became second nature for the team members.

"You play for me, you move, move, move!" he shouted as Angie and Melanie trudged toward batting practice. "You walk now, and you'll do it in the game. Speed and quickness will win for you just as often as skill." He clapped his long, thin hands in enthusiasm, then hopped back into the cart.

"Get me back to the outfield. I don't like the way those girls are picking up the ground balls," he said. "You leave me out there and come on back and do some batting practice pitching," he added. "I hate to see a big, strapping guy like you just sitting around all the time."

102

Kelli glanced at her youth leader and laughed at the trapped look on his face.

"Kelli, if you have time to stand around and listen to me talk to someone else, then you must need to do some more running," Herman snapped. This time, it was Jared's turn to laugh as Kelli scowled and took off for center field.

By Wednesday—short practice day due to church night—the girls were tired and cranky. Halfway through the workout, Mr. Hochman suddenly stopped practice and had Jared bring them all together near home plate. He nodded to the younger man, and Jared slid into the golf cart driver's seat and sped away, leaving the girls and Herman alone.

"Sit down. I got some things to say."

They flopped down on the infield grass while he remained standing, leaning slightly on an aluminum bat for support.

"Okay," he said with a growl. "I'm impressed. You wanted me to help out while your coach was gone, and I said I'd do it. For the past couple days, I've put you through the worst I could, because I wanted to see if you were really serious about wanting to win a championship. Maybe I've come down a little hard on some of you"—he glanced over at Kelli as he spoke—"but I did it to see if you had what it takes—to see if you could be coached. And," his voice dropped, "I did it to see if you really wanted an old geezer like me for a coach, or you were just saying so to make me feel good."

He allowed himself a little smile as the girls laughed.

"Well, like I said," he continued, "I'm impressed. I asked you to work your tails off, and you did it. Some of you get a mite feisty, especially those redheads at the corners." He nodded toward Sam and Mel, and again the team members laughed. "So," he said as the sound of the golf cart filled the air and Jared came wheeling back toward them. "I think this team is going to make the city of Fall River and the Comet teams of the past real proud." He nodded again. "Yep, real proud." He winked at them, and the girls cheered, suddenly not feeling tired anymore. "So, if you still want me to help, I'll be proud to do so."

They cheered again and jumped up.

"All the way to the championship!" Sam shouted, holding out her hand to Mr. Hochman, palm up. He stared at it for a couple of seconds, then grinned and slapped her hand. "Yeah!" she said with a roar while the rest of the girls cheered again.

Jared pulled to a stop and leaned on the steering wheel. "Well?" he asked.

"Guess it's a go," the old man responded.

"All right!" Jared yelled, punching his fist in the air. "After practice today, soft drinks are on me, down at Snyder's."

"Then let's do it right now," Herman said. "I think we've worked hard enough today. One more wind sprint and we go in."

"All the way out to the center field fence and back. Who's with me?" Darcy yelled. They all shouted and

104

clapped approval as Darcy led them out toward the fence on a joyous gallop.

"Wow, you've really got them fired up," Jared remarked.

"Even more than I was hoping," Herman said. "I was just going to have them run out to second base."

CHAPTER TEN

Friends

"THIS IS THE GREATEST THING SINCE SLICED BREAD," Marilyn Horner said. "I've never seen anyone improve the way Herman has since Kelli came in." She sighed and looked from Kelli to Jared, then glanced at the rest of the group. "But, kids, I can't sit here and tell you that each of you will have this kind of success with one of our residents.

"Kelli brought Mr. Hochman out of the doldrums, and he's become a happy, productive person again. But for most of you, if you decide to help us out, you'll find that the grandparent you adopt is not going to 'get up and go' like Herman has. On some days, they may not even get out of bed, and if they close the meeting with you by giving you a smile, you can consider it a big success. But they do need you. Many of them have no one else."

Jared looked around at the youth group. "Well, gang," he said, "you've heard about Angie's experience, and everyone in the community's heard about Kelli and Mr. Hochman." He waited for their laughter to subside. "Angie and Kelli are going to keep it going, and you may join them if you like."

Chad Pohlmeyer raised his hand. "I'd like to go for it," he said.

"Me, too," his friend Robert Jonas added.

Then the room was filled with voices, all saying yes. Marilyn's eyes filled with tears, and she turned away for a few seconds and wiped her eyes.

"You'll never know how much this means to me . . . to them. What it will mean for you someday."

Jared reached over and took her hand. "I think we do, and I'm sure that we will," he answered. "Maybe we can lead the way for other youth groups in this town to do the same thing."

"It really is amazing, the change in Herman," Marilyn said as she walked out to her car with Kelli and Jared at her side. "Has this experience meant as much to you, Kelli, as it has to him?"

"Yeah, I guess," Kelli groaned. "But I wish he wouldn't always pick on me at practice. If I don't do everything perfect, he acts like it's his fault."

"It's not that bad," Jared inserted.

"Yes, it is. Even the other girls have said so!"

The two adults stopped and stared.

"Well, they did," Kelli repeated, a defensive tone to her voice.

"I'm sorry if he's making things uncomfortable for you," Marilyn said. "Do you want us to reconsider this arrangement?"

Kelli shook her head. "It's okay. Hey, I'm glad he's doing great, and I really like talking to him—when we're not out there for practice. I just wish . . . oh, forget it. After all, I was the one who made such a big deal out of getting him out there to coach us."

"I really think he just wants you to succeed," Jared said. "I've talked with him after practice, and he's proud of you. I think he feels like he had a lot to do with your progress." Jared laughed. "He sees a lot of himself in you, Kelli, especially the way he was when he was your age."

"Well, I wish he didn't see it that way! He's not me! I'm me. I don't want to be exactly like him!"

Kelli's face flushed, and tears filled her eyes. She turned and ran down the street, leaving Jared and Mrs. Horner standing in stunned silence.

Thursday dawned gray and gloomy, matching Kelli's feelings as she dragged through breakfast and trudged off toward school. She had had a tough night, praying for guidance and understanding about how to deal with Mr. Hochman and herself. She was confused, and the overcast sky didn't help to lighten her self-imposed burden. She flipped open her history book and began reviewing her notes as she walked slowly along the sidewalk. About two blocks from the school, she paused at the corner to let the traffic clear, then jumped in surprise as a man's voice interrupted her thoughts.

"Going my way?"

Kelli closed the book and forced a small smile as Herman Hochman stood up from the concrete bench he had been sitting on and walked over to join her. He was still using his came, but she noticed that he wasn't walking as stiffly as he had a week before.

"Hi, Mr. Hochman. What are you doing out here?"

"Walking." He nodded at the bench. "And sitting."

"A little early for you to be out, isn't it?"

"When you get to be my age, any time you can go walking is a good time."

Kelli laughed.

"Thought I might find you on your way to school," he continued. "You won't mind walking a bit with me, will you?"

"Of course not. Why would I mind?"

"I had a talk with Marilyn last night," he said.

"Oh. I probably said some things I shouldn't have," Kelli responded. "Don't worry about it. I was just blowing off some steam."

He coughed nervously. "Well, I reckon you had a right. I thought it over some, and I've been pretty hard on you—harder than on the others. But I didn't do it to be mean, Kelli. I did it because I want you to succeed. I ain't got much to offer someone like you, except for what I got in my head." He reached up and tapped his forehead. "You know, an old coot like me's got a lot sittin' in there to share, and a lot of times we ain't got no one to share it with." He looked down at the ground. "For what you did for me, I wanted to do something back. I guess I didn't go about it very good."

Kelli pulled up and faced him, hugging her books tightly.

"What did I do for you?"

"Gave me back a reason to live," he said hoarsely.

"Oh." She let the word trail off as she watched a tear roll down his well-lined face. Her eyes grew hot, and she brushed at a tear of her own as he struggled to continue.

"You know, no one's ever asked me before to do what you asked. And when I decided to work with your team, I said to myself, 'That girl means more to me than anyone else I know. I'm going to work to help her be the best player in the whole region.' So . . . that's why I been pushin' at you, jawin' at you. I see so much in you, Kelli, and I don't want you to fail." He shuffled uneasily and stared back at the ground. "Never meant to sound mean. That's just my nature, I suppose. Guess that's why I never got married. No woman could stand my gruff ways."

He gave a wry laugh. "Sure proved them right, didn't I? Here I get a chance to do something good for one of the nicest, prettiest gals in Fall River, and all I do is end up having her hate me."

"Oh, no, Mr. Hochman, I don't hate you!" she exclaimed. Then she blushed. "And I'm not one of the nicest, prettiest girls in Fall River. If I were, I wouldn't have said mean things about you in the first place."

They stood looking at each other, an awkward silence filling the air.

"Maybe it would be best if I didn't keep coaching you

and your team."

"No!" Kelli shouted, then blushed again. "I-I mean, no. You can't quit. Not now. Not after all you've told us about not quitting or giving up. Besides, I may have been upset about you yelling at me, but I sure have learned a lot. If you quit now, I won't put the finishing touches on everything you've taught me." She set her jaw and glared at him. "You've got to promise to stay."

"All right, but only on one condition."

"What?"

"That you accept my apology, and we continue on as friends."

"Deal," she said firmly. She shifted her books under her left arm and extended her right hand. He stared at her hand for a few seconds before his face cracked into a broad smile and he warmly grasped her hand in his.

"You better get home and get some rest, and I better get to school. We've got a tough workout this afternoon if we expect to win that opening game with Point Pleasant."

"Go Comets!" he responded in his raspy voice. He leaned his cane against his side and clapped his hands together as he spoke.

"Yeah!" she yelled, holding out her right hand and exchanging a hand slap with her senior citizen mentor. She hurried off to class feeling the best she'd felt in weeks.

Behind her, Herman was grinning broadly as he watched her go.

The afternoon workout was barely a half hour old

when Herman blew his whistle and signaled for the team members to join him near home plate.

"Got a surprise for you," he said, glancing over his shoulder. "It's in there." He pointed to a bright orange bus pulling up to the field.

The girls craned their necks to see who it was. The bus door opened and ten girls wearing warmup uniforms and softball spikes clattered out and stood in a clump by the side of the bus. A large woman with an author-itative look on her face tromped over to where Herman and his team stood watching.

"Hi, old man!" she boomed, clapping him so hard on the shoulder that he nearly fell. "This the bunch you want us to test for you?" She gestured at the Comets and laughed.

"Ah, Rose. See you're as gentle as always," Herman answered. "This here's Rose Neiman. She runs the Y program over at South Park." He pointed at the girls by the bus. "Those there are probably the best ten players in that city who haven't had the good fortune to try out for a regular team. Rose takes 'em in off the streets and gives 'em some athletics to keep 'em busy. I thought it might be fun for you to play about three innings against 'em and see if you're as good as you think you are. Just a little pre-season scrimmage."

The Comets broke into excited chatter as Rose signal-ed for her girls to head out onto the field and start warm-ing up.

"You still playing any ball, Herman?" Rose asked. Then she answered her own question with a booming laugh. "Just joshin' you, old man." She looked at the Comet team. "You girls aren't letting this slave driver wear you out, are you? I've known old Herman for forty years, and he never does anything halfway. Don't know who talked him into helping your team, but my hat's off to the one who did, because he's the best around."

Kelli blushed as her team members all turned and looked at her. But Rose missed it, as she was already barking out instructions to her girls.

"Look, Herman, we'll be ready to go in a few minutes. I'll need a catcher. Otherwise we got all the positions covered." She winked. "I've got one of the best pitchers around, too. You sure three innings is enough? We'd be glad to go five for you if you'd like to see your girls try to get a hit. I don't think they can hit anything off her in just three innings."

The Comets erupted into a chorus of protests, and Herman held up his hands for them to be quiet.

"Thanks, Rosie, but three will be fine," he replied. "By that time your pitcher's going to be worn out from all the hitting we'll be doing."

The Comet players laughed in agreement, and Rose gave a mighty guffaw of her own before calling her team to get ready. Jared agreed to act as umpire, and ten minutes later the "game" was underway. Lara did the catching for the South Park girls, while Kelli settled comfortably into the catcher's role for the Comets.

After two innings, no one had scored, although the Comets had hit the ball hard and had three runners on base. Kari had pitched the first inning, Becky the second. Now Kari returned to pitch in the third. South Park's big first baseman stepped in to bat and promptly smashed the first pitch into the gap in right-center field, going all the way to second base before Darcy could recover the ball and keep her from advancing further. Kelli trotted out to the pitching rubber.

"Bear down and pitch it smooth and easy," she advised. "That girl can't score if you strike out the next three batters." She took the ball from Kari, smacked it into her glove for emphasis, then handed it back with a grin. "Bear down!"

She trotted back and settled in for the pitch. "Strike!" Jared made the call with a flourish from his umpiring spot and Kelli glanced over her shoulder at him before tossing the ball back.

"Showoff," she mumbled.

The batter struck out swinging on the next two pitches, and Kelli stepped out in front of the plate and gave Kari a thumbs-up sign as she tossed back the ball. Kari burned in the next two pitches, getting a swinging strike on the first, and another dramatically-called strike by Jared on the second. Kelli set her glove target on the outside edge of the plate, and Kari nodded and whipped the ball home, getting the batter swinging for her second strikeout.

Kelli went back to the pitcher's rubber as the lead-off batter returned and prepared to hit. "Those last two didn't have smooth swings," she advised, handing Kari the ball, "but this next girl is their lead-off hitter. I wouldn't be surprised to see her try to punch the ball into right field and get that runner around. Try to keep the ball on the inside edge of the plate. Okay?"

Kari nodded.

Her first pitch looked good, but Jared called it a ball and Kelli glared at him. He shrugged, but said nothing. The next pitch was way inside, nearly hitting the batter.

"Come on," Kelli yelled as she tossed the ball back. "Control! Control."

Kari went into her windup and threw a slow, sweeping curve, which started right at the batter, then broke toward the outside of the plate. The batter, though, refused to move and at the last second she swung, slapping the ball sharply into right. At the crack of the bat, the runner took off and already was coming around third when Darcy fielded the ball and threw it home.

Kelli glanced quickly at the runner, braced herself for a collision, and waited for the throw. The ball and the runner arrived simultaneously and, as Kelli turned to make the tag, she felt her feet go out from under her as the runner slid home. She fell with a thud, missing the tag.

"Safe!" Jared yelled, swinging his arms wide to make the signal. Kelli groaned while the girl punched her fist in the air with excitement and jumped up to receive a flurry of "high fives" from her teammates as she ran back to the bench.

The next batter hit a long fly ball to center field, but Darcy tracked it down and made the catch to end the inning. The Comets' half of the inning went fast—only five pitches—as Ray hit the first pitch right back to the first baseman, Kris hit a first-pitch fly ball that nearly went out of the park but was caught in a spectacular grab by the left fielder, and Becky struck out on three pitches.

As the South Rapids girls celebrated, the Comets lined up to shake hands, their heads down in defeat.

"Cheer up, girls," Rose boomed, walking over and shaking hands with each of them. "You've got a great team. I mean, we play all the time. I know they don't look it, but some of these 'girls' are in their twenties. Our pitcher did a couple years for a college team, and she said yours is one of the hardest hitting teams she's ever faced." She winked at Herman. "Old Herm knew all this, but he thought you could use a challenge. Good luck with your season!"

The girls brightened at her pronouncement and were even cheerier after Herman gathered them around him and dished out praise for their hitting and sharp play. "I think in a full game, you'd of beat 'em," he said. "So, go on in with your heads up. I think we got us one dynamite team!"

CHAPTER ELEVEN

Working In

R_AIN._

Kelli's bright outlook from Thursday faded fast as Friday turned darker and drearier. Now, with school out and the team gathered in the gymnasium, the gloom inside nearly matched that of outdoors.

"I hate rain," Becky said. The others murmured in agreement, looking toward Herman and Jared for their reaction.

"Now how can you hate rain?" Herman said. "Without it, this would be a pretty dull, dry old world, and that beautiful ball field you play on nothing more than a scraped off piece of ground."

"Well, that's not what I meant, exactly," Becky stammered. "It's just that we've got a game Tuesday, and now we can't even practice for it. What if it rains all weekend?"

"What if it does?" Herman asked. He looked around

at the group. "What's it going to hurt?"

The girls broke into a babble of excited chatter, telling Mr. Hochman exactly why it would hurt. He listened for a bit, then grinned and signaled for quiet.

"How many think it's raining today at Point Pleasant?"

They all raised their hands.

"That's what I was thinkin', too," he said. "You figure maybe they're out splashin' around in the mud trying to get some practicing done?"

"No way!" several of the girls shouted.

"They're a bunch of wimps over at Point Pleasant," Sam scoffed. "They don't even go out for practice when it gets a little cold."

"Is that right?" Jared said. "Wonder how they were able to beat you guys the past four years in a row?"

"Well, some teams have all the luck," she answered. "That doesn't mean they aren't wimpy." She smirked and the others laughed.

"Gee," Chappy said with a grimace, "if they're wimps, I wonder what that makes us?"

"Let's not talk about it," Ray replied.

"Well, I'd like to talk about it," Herman said. "Is that true? You lost four straight to Point Pleasant?"

The girls nodded sheepishly.

"And you always open the season with them?"

They nodded again.

Herman turned and looked out the window, where the rain was beating down. "Seems like rain always comes along about this time. What have you done in other years on rainy days?"

"Took the day off," Chappy said. "Can't work out when it's raining. We're usually pretty rusty when we get back outside."

"Hmmmm." Herman scratched his chin thoughtfully. "You know what I'm thinkin' is that when it rains, a big school like Point Pleasant doesn't take the day off."

"Oh, come on," Sam said incredulously. "They wouldn't be working out in this rain. No way." She shook her head as she spoke.

"Nope, not working *out*," he replied, "but maybe working *in*."

"What do you mean?" Kelli asked.

"I remember about twenty years ago when they built that new sports complex of theirs. Seems to me they included a spring sports workout area—indoors."

"But that's not fair," Kari said, jumping to her feet. "How are we supposed to compete against that?"

Mr. Hochman spread his hands wide and gestured toward the darkened gymnasium behind them. "Any reason why we can't play some catch in there? Anybody know how to turn on the lights?"

"I know Mr. Digby, the janitor," Kelli said. "I'm sure he'd turn them on for us."

"Go ahead and see if you can find him."

Kelli hurried off, and Herman turned back to the rest of the team. "We can wear tennis shoes in here for tossing the ball around, and maybe we can jury-rig something so we can try some other drills—like slidin' into home plate."

"Jury-rig," Sam said, puzzled. "What's that?"

He laughed. "Just an old farmer's expression. It means to rig something together to take the place of something you regularly would use." He gestured toward a pile of air bags that had been brought out for the track and field team. "I'll bet we could pile those up against one of the walls and practice sliding into them without hurting anybody. Might even be fun."

The lights began flickering on as Kelli came jogging back to the group.

"That reminds me," Herman added. "We can't forget about running. This old barn'll do just fine for a couple dozen wind sprints. Right after we do about ten laps around the outside of the basketball floor."

Jared chuckled as the team members groaned in unison.

"Before we start running, though, there's one other thing. We've got a little surprise." He exchanged a mysterious look with the younger man. "Suppose now's a good time for the surprise . . . or should we wait a while?"

"Now! Don't make us wait," the girls begged, looking from Herman to Jared and back again.

"Yeah, especially since we're not in any big hurry to start running," Rayanne implored.

"That's what I figured," Herman answered as the team members laughed. "Well, why not," he said with a grin. "I'm kind of anxious to share this surprise myself." He nodded to Jared, who hurried out into the rain. When he came back inside, dripping, he carried a

120

plastic-covered package.

"What's that?" Darcy asked, starting toward him.

"Hold it," Herman said firmly. "Everyone gather 'round here and sit down. Come on, hurry up." They hustled over and plopped down around him as Jared came to his side and handed him the package.

"This," Mr. Hochman exclaimed, pulling at the package and jerking out its contents, "is one of a dozen brand new shirts." He held up a bright red shirt with the word "Comets" slashed across the front in gold. On the back was a large gold number. As the girls oohed and ahhed in appreciation, he reached back into the sack and pulled out a cap, matching the one he had been wearing every day at practice.

"I sorta like 'em," he said, his voice filled with pride.

"You can thank Mr. Hochman for this," Jared offered, patting the older man on the shoulder. "He spent about two hours chewing on the sporting goods' store manager's ear. Got him not only to donate the shirts and caps, but to drive over to Greensboro and pick them up. He even knew the right guy to call over there to rush the order through, so you could all look pretty for your first game."

"Well, young man, I just figured that a bunch of champions ought to be dressed like champions," he said gruffly. "These here shirts ain't Big League or nothin', but they'll do. And when the season's over, you each get to keep your own shirt and cap. A little souvenir."

"Hey, thanks, Mr. H.," Darcy said. "These are fantastic!"

121

"Not only that, they're great!" Sam added. The other girls echoed their teammates' sentiments.

"Well, like I said, champions deserve good stuff. Your old uniforms were a disgrace.

"Now, come on!" Herman said, clapping his wrinkled hands enthusiastically. "Let's get to it. We may not have the facilities that Point Pleasant has, but I'll be darned if I'm going to let them be better prepared than my team—" He paused, his voice seemed to catch, and then he nodded. "*My* team," he said firmly. "I sorta like the sound of that, even if I've only got you for a few more days. What d'ya say, girls? Time to put Point Pleasant back in its place?"

They leaped up, cheering, and gathered around him. Even Jared moved in to clasp hands with the team members.

"What do you say, Comets?" Herman croaked, his voice cracking. "Let's make this the start of a championship year."

"Comets!" they screamed, then broke out and began their laps around the gym while Mr. Hochman and Jared began planning the "jury-rigged" home plate sliding zone.

It was still raining on Saturday, but Kelli didn't care. The Friday workout had been so productive that the entire team had left bubbling with enthusiasm. They weren't getting the chance to hit, but they had practiced precision throws, picking up ground balls—which bounced in even faster and harder than normal on the hard surface, and sliding into home plate to avoid the catcher's tag.

The home plate drill was loads of fun. The girls removed their shoes, started running from about sixty feet away, and then slid the final ten feet, first on their backs, then head first, and finally on each side. It reminded Kelli of summertime "slip-and-slide" in their neighbor's backyard. This didn't have any water, but the highly-polished basketball floor was almost as effective.

So today, when she awakened to the sound of rain beating on the roof, she just stretched, yawned, and smiled in anticipation. They had already decided on a Saturday practice, so it would be another day in the gym.

"Monday can be used for hitting," Kelli said aloud. It was a segment of the game that still concerned her, despite the fact that she had stood in and swung the bat without flinching since Mr. Hochman's "chewing out" earlier in the week.

She swung her feet out of bed and stood up, marveling at how good she felt. For the first time in three years, she was really in good shape. The achiness of the first days of practice had passed. Now she was fine-tuning her muscles and adding to her breathing capacity. At least that's how Coach McGuire had explained it to her when she had taken the coach's phone call last night and answered questions about the team's progress.

Kelli had mixed feelings about the coach coming back. She knew it was the woman's job, but she also wanted Mr. Hochman to remain. Maybe the old man could still help out once Coach McGuire returned. The coach's leg was healing nicely, she said, and she expected to rejoin the team by the end of next week. That meant Herman would coach during the opener against Point Pleasant and maybe even in the second game against Coopersville.

Just so they didn't let him down. Kelli worried about how he would take it if they played poorly. After all, he was old. Maybe he'd have a heart attack or something. Kelli shook her head. No sense in thinking bad thoughts. After all, wasn't he the best he'd been in years? That's what Mrs. Horner said.

"I'm getting nervous about the opener," Kelli told Angie as she jammed her things into her locker. It was nearly two-thirty, the time set for practice. Most of the team had already changed and headed to the gym.

"Not about . . . you know?" Angie said, touching her forehead just above the eye.

"No, nothing like that. More about doing well for Mr. Hochman. It's so important to him. Maybe even more than for us. After all, we've got school, our friends, lots of time ahead of us yet. He's got the team. That's it."

"No. He's got a lot more than that."

"What do you mean?"

"He's got a good friend. You." Angie grinned. "Now, let's not be late for practice or that friend's going to hit the roof. Then neither one of us will have to worry about playing softball, because we'll still be running extra wind sprints for punishment."

This indoor practice session was even better than Friday's. After an hour, as they lined up for wind sprints, the entire gymnasium suddenly brightened.

"Hey, look! The sun!" Becky yelled, pointing to the side windows. She sprang forward and did a cartwheel and then a back handspring in joy. The other girls clapped appreciatively at her demonstration and Herman, who had been frowning, changed his expression.

"A good sign, girls," he exclaimed. "If this weather clears up, we'll get two good days of drying before doing some batting practice on Monday." He hobbled stiffly over to the door and peered out. "Yes, indeed," he said cheerily. "A very good sign. Now I know we're going to be ready. Just seeing this sunshine makes me feel good all over." He beamed at the team, who stood expectantly at the starting line, still waiting to run.

"Do you feel so great that maybe you won't make us run these wind sprints?" Sam said cautiously. "I mean, watching all of us dying in here would be pretty depressing after seeing such a bright and cheery sight outdoors."

The other girls laughed and waited for Herman's reaction.

"Well, I tell you what. This change in weather makes me feel so happy that I'm going to stop practice early, so you can all go downtown with your friends to get a soft drink or something to eat."

They erupted into cheers and turned to go to the locker room.

"Girls!" he shouted.

They stopped and looked back.

"Right after we finish this last set of wind sprints."

They groaned and trudged back to the starting line.

"I'm happy," Herman said with a shrug. "I didn't say I was nice, too."

Chapter Twelve

Panic

KELLI WAS STILL SAVORING THE AFTER-PRACTICE gab session with her friends when she got the call from her brother, Tommy. He was coming home on Sunday in time to join the family for church and could stay all the way through Tuesday night before he had to head back to campus.

"Sunday through Tuesday?" Kelli gave a squeal of delight. "But what about your Monday and Tuesday classes?"

"The college is giving us two full days to work out next year's course schedules with our advisors. That way there shouldn't be so much confusion when we go through pre-registration in May."

"So? Don't you have an advisor?"

Tom laughed. "Yes, I have an advisor. But I've already worked out my schedule for next year, and my advisor approved it before we finished the winter term. Since

I've got everything under control, I can do whatever I want with those two days."

"So you're coming home! Great!"

"Oh, and Eric says hello, too," Tom said. "You must really have him under a spell. I hear more about my sister from him than I do from Mom and Dad."

"Come off it." Kelli's face turned red.

"And stop blushing, Kel," he said.

"How do you know I'm blushing?"

"Because I know my baby sister," he replied. "Don't worry. Eric's great, and I'm glad you're going out with him. Any other special guys I should know about?"

"Just Herman."

"Herman. Who's Herman?"

"I'll tell you all about him when you get home," she said. "Really, he's the sweetest guy."

"Does Eric know about Herman?" Tom said suspiciously.

"Of course he does."

"This sounds too complicated for a phone conversation," her brother answered. "I'll expect a full report tomorrow."

Sunday was a picture postcard, early spring day, and Kelli felt absolutely glorious as she dressed for church and waited for Tommy to arrive. It was amazing how much she missed him since he had gone off to college— when he lived at home, the two of them had bickered most of the time.

They celebrated Tommy's homecoming with dinner out after church. After Tom had filled them in on his southern trip, Kelli talked non-stop about the softball team.

"Sounds like this guy Herman occupies all your thoughts," Tom said as they rode home. "Eric's going to be mad."

Kelli stretched her foot across the back seat and kicked him in the shin.

"Ow," he said. "Mom! Kelli's kicking me!"

"Honestly," their mother said with a sigh. "I haven't missed that!"

"So, you really do have a thought or two left for Eric, huh?" Tom teased.

Kelli blushed. "From time to time," she responded.

"That's good," he answered as they turned into their driveway. "Otherwise he would've been real disappointed that he came all this way."

Kelli gasped as the tall, red-haired boy stood up from where he was sitting on their front step and gave them a little wave.

"Guess who else was smart enough to work out next year's course schedule in advance," Tom said with a chuckle. "You know," he continued, puffing out his chest, "I'm such a good influence on Eric, I can hardly stand it. Having me for a roommate has been a great thing for him." He laughed and ducked as Kelli tried to give him a shove.

"I wanted to have some time to talk to my little sis," he went on, "but far be it from me to stand in the path of true love. I just couldn't say no when he asked to come along." Tommy reached down and rubbed his shin. "Now you take it easy on him, Kel. He doesn't know how violent you can get." He dodged out of her way again, then yanked open the car door and bailed out before she could reach him.

The afternoon spent with Eric and the evening spent talking with her brother seemed far too short, especially so when the Monday morning alarm clock brought her back to the realities of the salt mine known as school. It also seemed grossly unfair when Tom wished her a sleepy "good day" as he rolled over in his bed to sleep a couple more hours.

"I paid my dues last year," he said cheerily as she grumbled about the injustice. "Study hard, little sister, and you too can graduate and go on to bigger and better things . . . like sleeping late."

Just on general principle, Kelli threw a pillow at him before darting out the door.

But once she got going, the day held an air of excitement. There was just one more day till the first game, and Kelli found herself filled with the nervous energy and feeling of excitement she had always known at the start of a new season. She realized just how much she had missed being a part of it in the past two years.

"It's good to be back!" she shouted to no one in particular as she raced out into the practice field after school. Without even waiting for her teammates, she jogged twice around the field, urging the others to get going.

"Kelli, you make me tired," Mel complained. "You

keep that up and we'll be sending another delegation to see you—this time to ask you to *leave* the team."

Kelli just laughed and soon had all her teammates in an enthusiastic mood for their final day of practice.

The warm-ups went quickly; then they took batting practice with Jared alternating between Kari and Becky as the girls pounded out hit after hit. Kelli swung the bat with new-found confidence, zeroing in on each pitch and slamming it hard into the outfield. Finally Herman blew his whistle and called the team members together at home plate.

"Time to try out some of those slides we worked on indoors," he told them. "Kelli, get your catcher's gear on and Jared, you do the batting. We'll put people into their usual fielding spots, and the pitchers can run first. I want each girl to start at third and head for home at the crack of the bat. Whoever fields the ball, fire it home. I want to see how well you slide to avoid Kelli's tag."

Kelli strapped on her shin pads and hurried over to her catcher's spot, taking a quick throw from Chappy and tossing it back as they waited for Jared to take a couple of practice swings.

"Think you can hit it out of the infield?" Kelli said under her breath as he stepped over to the plate.

"You kidding? If I wanted to I could hit nothing but home runs," he sniffed. "But Herman wants the infield to practice throwing the ball home, so I'll hold back and hit ground balls."

"Hah," Kelli laughed. "Mr. Hochman saved you from embarrassing yourself." She reached up and tapped him on the arm.

"Get ready to run in to catch the ball," she yelled at her teammates. "Grandpa here is doing the batting." She turned quickly and glanced at Mr. Hochman. "No offense," she added.

Herman moved over closer to the plate. "You were talking about him, not me, right?"

"Yeah."

"All right, then. I've seen him hit, and I think he hits like my grandfather, too."

The girls roared in laughter.

"Great," Jared said in mock despair. "I put my heart and soul into this for you girls, and what do I get? Disrespect. It's a good thing I'm such a kind and understanding guy, or I'd be hurt by all this talk about my wimpy batting style. Besides," he added, pretending to ripple his muscles, "I haven't shown you the real me . . . yet." He held the bat out with his right hand and posed like a muscle-builder as the girls whistled and raved.

Jared nodded, tossed the ball into the air, and promptly swung and missed. "Just seeing if you were alert," he said.

For the next few minutes he rapped out several hits as the outfielders and pitchers took turns racing home and trying to avoid Kelli's tag.

"Okay, now you try the slide, Kelli, and Lara, you do the catching," Mr. Hochman said. Kelli jogged out to third base while Lara strapped on the shin pads and chest protector.

"Hey, Kelli!" Sam called from her first base position. "Better make it good. Look who's watching!"

Kelli peered in the direction Sam was pointing and smiled, then waved. Eric and Tom were leaning up against the fence in front of the first base bleachers. Both boys waved in return.

"Remember to slide to the back side of the plate, Kel," Mel offered. "Most of the throws have been coming in short, and you had to reach out over the plate to get them."

Kelli nodded and stared toward the plate. Jared tossed the ball high in the air and smacked it hard, right back toward third base. Kelli was off like a shot, tearing down the base line, while Melanie hustled over to make the grab and throw the ball home. As Kelli approached the plate, she saw Lara stiffen, waiting for the throw. Then, suddenly, she saw her straighten up and leap high into the air. Behind her, Herman held up both hands in self-defense. A look of fear came over his face as Lara began to step backward, right into him.

"Lara, stop!" Kelli screamed, holding up on her preparation to slide. "Don't step back!"

Too late. Lara stepped directly onto the old man's right foot, her cleats sinking into his soft shoe. Together they tumbled to the ground.

Jared tossed the bat aside and leaped to the pair as Tom and Eric raced around the protective screen toward them.

Herman groaned, clutching at his leg, as Jared lifted Lara away from him.

133

"Mr. Hochman, Mr. Hochman, are you all right?" Kelli dropped to her knees beside him, looking helplessly at the anguish on Herman's face.

Eric scrambled in beside her, glanced at Herman's leg, and then leaned toward him. "Is it your knee or your leg?" he asked, slipping both hands beneath the old man's leg. It was twisted grotesquely toward one side.

"My leg," he moaned. "I-I can't feel it." He started to sit forward, then gasped and fell back, unconscious.

"Oh, no!" Kelli gasped. "Oh, God, no! Please let him be all right! Please," she prayed, clasping both hands tightly, "please don't let him die."

CHAPTER THIRTEEN

Coach

"ALL RIGHT, I'LL BAT WARM-UP FOR YOU AND BE ON the bench if you need me. But it's going to be up to you to do it on your own, you know?"

Jared looked around the locker room where the girls sat quietly, dressed in their bright new shirts, looking both nervous and disillusioned. Becky snuffled loudly, and a tear rolled down her cheek before she could brush it away.

"Don't worry, okay?" Jared added.

"How can we not worry?" Becky asked. "How can we go out there and play a game while Mr. Hochman's lying hurt in the hospital? For all we know, he might be dying."

"I doubt the man is dying of torn ligaments," Jared said dryly. "He may be hurting, but he's not dying."

"Well, we're really worried about him," she answered. "How can we play well when we're worried?"

Jared walked to the center of the room and faced the team. "You've got two choices, gang. You can feel sorry for yourselves, hang your heads, and go out there and hand over all your hopes and dreams to Point Pleasant. Or, you can go out there, take all the God-given talents that you have, and combine them with the skills that that old man has helped you develop to their fullest during the past ten days." He took a couple of steps toward the door, stopped and turned back.

"You put your trust in Herman Hochman to help you through a difficult time, and he gave you all he had. The best thing you can do for him is to go out and prove that what he did wasn't done in vain." He sighed and shook his head. "You may go out there and lose today, but if you do, I hope you can say it was because they were better than you—not because you didn't try your hardest and do your best.

"Put some faith in God, too. He's given each of you your athletic abilities, and He sent Mr. Hochman to help you through a real difficult time. Mr. Hochman may not be here, but God's here if you put your faith and trust in Him."

The girls sat silently for several seconds after Jared turned and left.

"Well?" Kari asked, glancing at her teammates.

"Deep subject," Sam replied. There was a snicker from Mel, then Krissie started laughing and Kelli joined in.

"Let's go win this one for Mr. Hochman," Rayanne said.

They stood and crowded together.

"I'd like to say a prayer before we go out," Kelli said.

The other girls murmured their agreement and they all clasped hands and bowed their heads.

"Lord," Kelli began, "a good friend of ours is hurt today and needs your help. Be with him, Lord, and be with us to help us play our best game. Keep us safe and help us to play to the best of our abilities. Amen."

She looked up and held her hand out in the middle of the circle. The others reached in and stacked their hands on hers. "Okay, Comets, let's go win this one for Herman."

"For Herman!" they shouted. Then they erupted from the locker room and headed for the field.

As they rounded the corner of the building and turned toward the ball diamond, Becky suddenly stopped and pointed. "Can you believe it!" she exclaimed.

There, just behind the wire fence which ran behind the home team's bench, sat Mr. Hochman and Coach McGuire. Each was propped in a lawn chair with a pile of foam rubber mattresses in front to support an injured leg. Each was dressed in the Comets' bright colors, wearing a red cap with the yellow-gold C in the center. A bright red blanket was draped across their laps.

Behind them, filling up a large share of the home team's bleachers, were the members of Kelli and Angie's youth group, each sitting beside a resident of Herman's senior citizen home. Standing prominently in the midst of the group, which broke into cheers at the sight of the

Comet team, were Eric and Tom. First the team members laughed, then they reacted to the cheers with cheers of their own and ran to join the group.

Crowding around their two coaches, the girls all began asking questions at the same time, until finally Coach McGuire shouted for quiet. She nodded to Herman, who looked fondly at the team members before speaking in a raspy, emotion-filled voice.

"There weren't no way I coulda missed this game, ya know," he said. "I might not be feelin' good enough to stand out there beside you, but I can sit back here and jaw at ya some, so's you'll get irritated and do good." He chuckled and the girls smiled. "After all, ain't that why you do so good when I'm around? 'Cause I get on your nerves all the time?"

The team members laughed.

"That's the truth, too," Mel explained to Coach McGuire. "He has a way of getting on you when you mess things up, and all you want to do is get out there and prove that he's wrong. It's great!"

"That's great?" she responded. "Hmmm, I may have to change my coaching techniques."

"Well," Herman growled, gesturing toward the stands behind him, "I brought all your friends and half of mine along, so I hope you girls aren't going to just stand all day talkin'. I see Point Pleasant ain't wastin' no time, and they don't look too slouchy either." Then he glanced over at Coach McGuire and held a wispy hand in her direction. She reached across and clasped it, and suddenly all the team members were doing the same. "You

138

can do it, girls," he said gruffly. "Comet power!"

"Comet power!" they yelled, then broke for their fielding positions as Jared picked up a bat and ball and went to hit to them. Kelli started for her catcher's gear, then stopped and walked back.

"Listen," she said, facing Mr. Hochman. "I-I just want you to know that—"

He reached out and took her hand. "I already know," he said. "I want you to know that I feel the same way."

She stepped closer and gave him a warm hug, then patted the coach on her shoulder. "We're going to get this one for you, Coach," she glanced back down at Herman. "For both of you."

"That's good," Coach McGuire replied, "because I've asked Mr. Hochman to give me a hand for the rest of the season, once that leg of his heals up a bit. He tells me that won't be much more than a week, if he has anything to say about it."

"Really? Terrific!" Kelli exclaimed.

"Now get going," Herman said. "The game's going to be half over before you get out on the field."

While the girls went through warm-ups, the coaches went over the lineup card and arranged them in batting order. When Kelli saw the lineup, with Kris as the lead-off batter and herself batting last, her face dropped.

"We put you last because you've been out a couple of years," Coach McGuire said quickly. "We know you can hit, Kelli, but we want you to get into the game a bit before we put you up to bat. You understand?"

Kelli swallowed hard and nodded.

"Give us a couple good games, then you'll move up," the coach added.

The girls gathered around for final instructions while the Pointers went through their infield and batting drills.

"Everybody set?" Sam asked, staring straight at Kelli as she spoke.

They murmured their readiness, but Kelli kept silent, determinedly buckling her shin guards into place. As Point Pleasant cleared the field, Kelli stood, strapped on the last of her catcher's gear and cleared her throat.

Her teammates grew silent. "I-I just want to say a couple words before we go out there." She toed the ground nervously. "A few weeks ago, I had given up on myself and my abilities. But you," she gulped, "you never gave up on me—either as a friend or as a player. Then I met this guy." She leaned over and gave Herman's shoulder a squeeze. "And between him and all of you and strength from God, I've got something back I thought was gone forever." Her eyes grew misty, and she stopped to regain her composure. Looking up, she saw that some of the other girls' eyes also were glistening. "So I just wanted to tell you that, win or lose today, I'll always be grateful for this chance. I promise to give you a great season and make you proud of me."

"We're already proud of you, Kelli," Sam said, reaching out and clasping her friend's hand. "But, uh—," she paused. "We'll really be proud if you get a couple of hits, drive in a couple of runs, and score a couple of times, too." She grinned at the others. "Right, gang?"

"That's why we asked her to come out, isn't it?" Darcy asked.

"I thought it was because she was our friend," Kari said.

"Sshhh," Chappy cut in. "Don't tell her."

"Oh, for crying out loud!" Kelli laughed. "This is the hardest bunch to try to say anything nice to."

"Yeah, we haven't got time for all this sentimental stuff," Ray announced. "We've got a ball game to take care of." She tried to say it gruffly, but her grin gave her away, and she came over to give Kelli a big hug. "Glad to have you back on the team, Kel."

One by one the girls stepped in to hug Kelli. The last one was Angie.

"Thanks, Ang."

"For what?"

"Just thanks. You've always been there as a best friend, and I couldn't have ever asked for better."

"Even when I helped gang up on you to get you back on the team?"

"Especially then," Kelli said. She spun around to her teammates. "Hey, everybody! I'm inspired. Let's do it to the Pointers!" They clasped hands one more time. "Win or lose," Kelli said, "this is the best team in the world!"

As they broke from the huddle onto the field, Kelli stopped and looked into the bright, clear sky. "Well, God," she said softly, "thanks." She put her catcher's mitt onto her left hand, then turned and gave a "thumbs up" sign first to Mr. Hochman, then to her brother and

Eric in the stands.

"Play ball!" yelled the umpire. Taking a deep breath and savoring the smell of a perfect spring day, Kelli pulled the catcher's mask into place and trotted confidently toward home plate.